I0552837

WHAT'S DONE in the Dark

MYRANDA RAE

WHAT'S DONE IN THE DARK

THE UNDERWORLD DUOLOGY
BOOK ONE

MYRANDA RAE

Publisher: Myranda Rae

Publication date: April 2022

Author: Myranda Rae

Email: connect@myrandarae.com

Website: myrandarae.com

Please direct all inquiries to the author.

ALSO BY MYRANDA RAE

Contemporary

When I Whisper His Name

Unplanned

Lewd & Lascivious

The Void He Fills

Pink

Paranormal/Shifter

Beast

Hardest to Love

Alphas, Kings & Playthings

ABOUT THE AUTHOR

A bonafide motha' to five kids under the age of eight, Myranda requires no fewer than 2 cups of black coffee (2 sugars) each day to support her habits and has finally built up the courage to publish her work. She enjoys noise-cancelling headphones and long waits in school pick-up lines and can change a diaper one-handed while blindfolded.

CHAPTER 1

ane

I FUCKING HATE GROVELING. Nothing makes my trigger finger itch quite like the sight of a grown man reduced to a whimpering mess, begging for his miserable life. It's pathetic. But what disgusts me more is how often they think it'll work.

"How much do you owe me?" I don't need to ask; I already know.

The sniveling worm chokes through his sobs, "Twenty thousand." He sucks in a breath, his gaze glued to me as I stand.

"Why were you gambling at Hanzos?" A hot ball of anger is moving up my chest. "Did you think I didn't know about that?" His ignorance would be amusing if it weren't so infuriating. "You lost nine thousand there just last night."

"I... I thought-"

"You thought that I was too fucking stupid to keep tabs

1

on you!" My voice is calm as I grab ahold of his wet, disgusting face. "That was my money you lost last night, the money you owed to me."

"I'm sorry, Kane. Please, I need more-"

"If you say 'time,' I'm going to blow a hole through your skull. You've had six months. Where the fuck is my money?" I press my fingers into his cheeks, squeezing.

"I can get it to you by Friday."

"And how do you plan to do that? Sell organs on the black market? You useless fucking waste of space."

"M-My wife can dance at The Playground! She can-"

His whining voice is silenced by my loud laughter.

"You're offering me your wife?" Unbelievable. If I thought he was useless before—now I'm sure.

"Yes, I heard that some people transfer their debts-" The deafening bang of my Glock silences the room. I'm done with this conversation. I'm done with him.

Wiping a drop of blood spatter from my cheek, I turn to the group of trembling men lined up waiting for their own judgments.

"What the fuck was he talking about?"

One of my enforcers shuffles slightly on his feet, and the ever-present calm rage starts to boil in my veins.

"What the fuck was he talking about?" I annunciate each word.

The room is silent enough to hear the thumping hearts of everyone quietly praying I don't call them forward.

"You," I point to an older man in the back. My enforcer grabs his arm and drags him forward.

"Tell me what the fuck he was talking about and I'll spare you, no questions asked."

"When someone dies, the debt moves to one of their

family members. People transfer debts to pay them off faster, wives, daughters." The man's voice shakes.

My finger moves over the trigger as I turn to my men. No one will make eye contact. These mother fuckers.

"You," I point to the man, "get the fuck out of here. My men… who authorized this? I feel I have been very clear, debtors pay their debts, not their families. That fucking spineless rat was trying to shift his debt over to his wife."

No one speaks, no one makes eye contact.

Pulling the trigger twice, two large bodies hit the floor.

"Who!" My voice booms through the room.

"Zion, Sir." Someone finally says.

Of course, he did. I knew it was him. No one else would defy me. I just wanted someone to speak up and say it.

"It stops today. Clean up this mess, now."

Leaving the trembling crowd with my men, I walk briskly from the marble hall.

It looks like it's time to pay my little brother a visit. Thunder rumbles in the night sky as the first raindrops land on my shoes.

"The Playground," I nod to Declan as he pulls the car door open for me.

"Right away, sir."

The grimy city streets flash past the windows as he expertly maneuvers the back alleys and side streets.

Pouring whiskey into a crystal glass from the backseat bar, I let the warm burn quell my rage.

The twinkling neon lights of The Playground illuminate the dark, reflecting off of the wet asphalt.

As usual, there is a line of drunk, disorderly men outside waiting to get inside to pay for the privilege of watching naked women gyrate on stage.

3

Stepping out of the open door, I nod to Dec, "Wait nearby. I won't be here long."

"Yes, Sir."

As the bouncer opens the velvet ropes for me to enter, I note my men standing quietly in line. The loud, obnoxious noise, gone.

"As you were, gentlemen, it's your night off."

The hooting and hollering echo through the street as the door closes behind me.

Animals, all of them.

A fully nude woman is on the end of the stage in a full split, her ass shaking to the loud music. I look past her for my brother. Where is that stupid fucker? I would like to get out of here as quickly as possible.

"Gentlemen, get your dollars ready!" His voice blasts through the speakers, "Buttercup has a special show for you tonight!"

I finally spot him at the sound booth as 'Buttercup' slinks across the stage.

Beckoning him with one finger, I walk through the door behind the bar toward his office. The two-way glass window in his office gives a clear view of the stage. Sitting on the stiff leather couch, I watch Buttercup's "special show."

Leaning back, I close my eyes. There is nothing special about this show. A naked bitch dancing on a pole, the same as every other.

"Kane!" Zion enters the room loudly, my moment of peace ruined.

I stand and stare at him with folded arms.

"What?"

"You know what."

He thinks for a moment, "Is this about that fucker I shot yesterday? Look, man, he was coming after me!"

"No. That's not what this is about. Who did you shoot?"

"Oh, just some guy. I was fucking his wife, and he had the nerve to show up here and burst into my office!"

I chuckle, "Yeah, no, I don't give a fuck about that."

"Then what?"

"I've been informed that you're taking debt transfers again. I hate that shit. It stops now, tonight. Anyone who is paying a debt for someone else finishes the night, and tomorrow you will have to find new dancers. I don't care what you have to do to get your money back from the fucker you lent it to, but don't let them switch that shit over."

He rolls his eyes. "Yeah, yeah, OK."

"Stop fucking doing it or I'll shoot you."

A wide grin splits his face. "That's what you said last time."

CHAPTER 2

 naïs

DRIP, drip, drip.

My heart is pounding in my ears. Each step into the alley makes bile rise in my throat. I'm not supposed to be here, he told me to wait in the car.

When four men walked back out onto the street and he wasn't with them, I knew something bad had happened. I didn't hear gunshots, so I'm holding out hope that he's alive.

My feet crunch over broken glass, and I freeze. It's eerily quiet aside from the constant drip.

The flicker of the streetlight casts shadows on the building beside me. Each time something moves, I panic only to have it be nothing.

The air is damp and foggy, and the rain is falling like a mist now. The delicate drizzle has soaked me down to the skin, leaving me shivering.

6

Trampled cardboard and bags of trash are piled high on either side, making the walkway narrow. When I reach the dumpster at the end, I'm gripped with fear. Inhaling a shaky breath, I pull up on my toes to peek inside.

Trash. It's full of trash.

The momentary relief I feel is short-lived. A groan draws my attention to a pile of garbage on the other side of the dumpster.

"Dad?"

As I cautiously approach the sound, my heart pounds in my throat. As I move one of the bags, I see his hand.

"Oh, God, dad!" Tossing the bags to the side, I move them enough to see his face.

"Anaïs, run," he coughs, and blood dribbles down his chin.

"I can't leave you here!" Even if I wanted to run, my body won't go. Every muscle in my body is tight, coiled in fear, too tense to move.

"Go," he chokes out.

"Let me help you, I'll get you home," I try to stop the bleeding, but it appears to be coming from everywhere. I keep pressing down on the bloody open wounds, but it's a useless effort.

"Anaïs, run," his voice is stern. If he wasn't so gravely injured, I would fear my punishment for disobeying.

Tears burn and blind my eyes as I stand on shaky legs. I want to stay for a moment to say our goodbyes. The words are all clogged in my throat. A painful ball of emotion is stuck there, blocking my attempt to speak.

As I take a step away, his breathing changes; the harsh, labored breaths are suddenly quiet. Against his orders, I watch his chest instead of running. There is no movement.

I don't need to check. He's dead. In my heart, I know it.

The streetlight flickers and breaks my transfixed gaze.

7

With the quietest steps I can manage over the gravel and glass, I run toward the opening at the other end of the alley.

Dad's car is parked just across the street. Stepping onto the sidewalk, I collide with the solid chest of a very large man.

Falling backward I brace myself for impact with the ground, but it doesn't come. The man has me by the arm, holding me suspended in midair.

He's not alone. The equally large man behind him smiles down at me. The kind of smile that makes my stomach roll.

"Hello, love! We were just looking for you," his blood-stained hand wraps tightly around my mouth, and he pulls me from the other man's grip.

I thrash and struggle, but it's no use. The blunt handle of his gun comes down over my head, causing my vision to blur before going completely black.

Everything is hazy for a moment, just darkness and confusion. Then I remember.

Jolting forward, I sit up and open my eyes. The sudden movement and brightness of the room make me wince. Nauseous and dizzy, I drop my head back down.

"You're awake!"

I crack one eye open to find the origin of such a cheery voice.

The girl standing in front of me is naked except for two small heart-shaped stickers over her breasts.

"Let me go get Zion!"

Before I have a chance to say anything, she's bouncing out of the room.

With a groan, I force myself to sit up again. I'm on a filthy, itchy plaid sofa in the corner of a small room. There are racks of bikinis, if they could even be classified as such, lining one wall. A small desk with a mirror is pushed against the other wall.

Make-up, hygiene products, condoms, clear plastic heels, and articles of clothing are thrown all around the room.

The door swings open, and the same girl skips inside. An intimidatingly large man follows behind her.

As soon as I get a look at his face, my pulse quickens. The girl said his name earlier, but it didn't register.

Zion Azrael. The devil's little brother.

He would be almost impossible not to recognize due to his stature and tattoos, but one, in particular, gives him away.

Damned. Inked under his eye on his right cheek.

I'm glad I'm sitting down. My legs are trembling, so I'm not sure I would be able to stand.

"Hello, babydoll." He sits beside me on the sofa with a smile that sends a chill up my spine. It's sweet, kind even; that's what scares me. My father told me all about him, I know what horrors hide behind his handsome face.

"Do you know why you're here?" His voice is almost soft, as if he knows a harsh word would crack my already thin composure.

Not trusting my voice, I shake my head.

"Your father owed me a large sum of money. Now that he's departed, I need to recoup that somehow. Do you understand where this is going?"

I nod my head again.

"Good girl. You will work here, at The Playground, until I am satisfied that the debt is repaid."

I don't know what The Playground is, but I can guess based on the mostly naked girl behind him.

"The harder you work, the more money you earn, the faster the debt will be paid, and you will be free to leave. Do you understand, babydoll?"

Turning to the girl, he stands, "show her around, get her settled in, then get your ass back out there."

When he's gone, she sits down beside me. My fingers gently prod the throbbing wound just inside of my hairline.

"I'm Kelly," she pulls me up to stand, "my stage name is Honey. Sounds like you're going to be called Babydoll."

I stumble slightly as I follow her out the door and across the hall to another room. This one is almost identical except it's empty aside from the furniture.

"This will be your room. Do you have anything with you?"

"W-Wait, am I not allowed to go back to my house?"

"No, you live here now."

Lunging forward, I fall to my knees in front of a small plastic trash can. My stomach heaves, forcing up the small amount of food I ate today.

By the time I stop retching, my face is covered in tears and sweat.

I stay down on my knees, holding my pounding head as I sob into my hands.

"Look, I won't sugarcoat this. I don't know how much you owe, but you're probably going to be here for a while. No use crying. Get up and start working, Zion is fair. You can keep half of your tips for personal expenses, or you can give him eighty percent to get out faster. Work hard, keep your head down, and stay out of trouble. It's not too shabby."

"What do I have to do?"

"There are several jobs. You can dance, that's what I do. It makes the most money. You can serve drinks or you can clean. If you clean you have to work out wages with Zion, but trust me, you don't want to do that. This place is filthy, and the pay is shit!"

"How long have you been here?"

"A year. My debt should be paid off in three months, but I'm going to stay on as a hired dancer."

My throat closes up, and I feel like I'm choking. A year?

"Come on, let me show you around so I can get back to work."

She stands up and studies me with furrowed brows.

"You can't wear that. Follow me."

CHAPTER 3

 naïs

"I-I CAN'T. No way! I can't wear that!"

She's holding out a piece of string with two tiny triangles in the middle of it.

"Why not? It will fit you." She holds one of the triangles up over my chest.

"No! I can't. Is there- Do you have something that's a little bit... more?" I gesture over my body.

She hums and runs her fingers over the almost nonexistent scraps of fabric in front of her.

"Come here," she takes my hand and pulls me out and down the hallway to a room with "Cinnamon" written on a piece of tape stuck to the door.

"Cin? We've got a new girl, and she needs something to wear." She taps on the door.

I'm startled as it flies open—a naked woman stepping out.

"Ten percent of your tips tonight, and you can have anything you want." A smile spreads over her lips. Not a kind smile, but a slick one.

Honey rolls her eyes but follows her into the room.

"Deal?" She puts her hands on her hips and taps her foot impatiently.

She has some things that look like they might cover me somewhat.

"Yes, deal." I don't have a choice but to accept her terms.

"I'll be coming to collect when my shift is over. I've got to go," she checks her lips in the mirror before rushing out.

"Please, hurry," Honey sounds anxious.

I look over the rack, my brain unable to make a decision.

"What about this?" She holds up a sheer pink camisole with the smallest panties I've ever seen.

"I, ok, sure." I grab it and, with shaking fingers, start to undress. My plain gray t-shirt and jeans are suddenly prized possessions that I wish to never part with.

"You can't go out there like that," she points at my body, "you can't have any hair."

Yes, ok, this is definitely hell. Too bad you can't actually die from embarrassment, or I would be free from this situation.

"Look, go to the bathroom down the hall and ask for Lindy; she'll get you fixed up. I'll be watching for you. When you come out, I'll show you around."

She takes my hand and pulls me out into the hallway, pointing to the bathroom door as she quickly leaves me.

"H-Hello? Lindy?" I call into the bathroom.

"Who are you?" A woman stands up from an armchair, cigarette smoke clouding the air.

13

"I'm Babydoll, I'm new. Honey sent me to find you." The name is rancid on my tongue.

"Ah," she nods and gestures to a plastic card table set up in the middle of the floor, "lay down, I'll have you out of here in ten minutes."

True to her word, she had me waxed as bare as the day I was born in no time at all. She wiped away the blood that had dried on my forehead and put a first aid cream on the gash. She also administered a birth control shot. I guess she's a jill of all trades.

With tender skin, I make my way down the long hallway. The camisole is so short and see-through. I keep pulling it down, trying to cover more of myself, but there's not enough fabric.

The door at the end of the hallway might as well be a three-headed demon. I'm walking so slowly that it might take me the rest of tonight just to make it there. I don't want to go out there. The fear and anxiety are like pressure in my chest. I can't take a breath. My vision is blurry, and my heart is pounding into my ribs so hard it's painful.

When I reach the door, I have to choke down air as best I can to keep from throwing up.

I lean my forehead onto the wood, forcing my emotions down. I don't have a choice, I have to do this.

The door opens from the other side, the loss of support sending me forward onto the ground.

"Babydoll!" I feel a hand on my arm. "I was just coming to look for you, are you alright?"

"No." Bile starts to rise in my throat as I panit. "I want to clean, I'll be a cleaner, I can't do this!"

A small crowd has gathered around us now, mostly men, loud and laughing. Honey's face is sympathetic as she helps me up and leads me toward the bar.

"Let's go see if Zion is free."

A door behind the bar leads us to a narrow staircase. She knocks at the door at the top of the stairs.

"Come in." His voice booms over the loud music downstairs.

I gasp, shocked, and horrified when we step into the room. Zion is sitting behind his desk, a naked woman sitting on his lap, facing us. The girl bounces up and down on top of him. She doesn't stop or try to cover up, it's like she doesn't notice us.

"What do you need?" His voice is tight.

"Babydoll wants to clean."

"We don't need any more cleaners, sorry, Babydoll," he grunts and starts rubbing his hand between the woman's legs. She moans loudly and bounces faster.

I'm blushing, heat burning in my cheeks as I try not to watch them.

"Come on," Honey grabs my hand and pulls me out of the room, closing the door quickly behind her. "I'll introduce you to Coco the bartender. You can be a cocktail waitress."

"Do I still have to wear this?"

"No." She cringes. "But I get the feeling you won't like the waitress uniform either." She hooks her arm in mine and walks me toward the crowded bar. "Coco?" She yells over the vibrating bass toward a woman making drinks. She's wearing a bodysuit made of three leather straps that sit on her chest, covering nothing. Another strap comes down between her legs like a loop, connecting behind her to the chest straps.

"Is that the uniform?" I mumble to myself as the woman makes her way toward us.

"This is Babydoll. She's going to be your new server."

"The tables start at one and go up to fifty. Each section is

15

divided up between the servers. You can take this area near the bar for tonight," she yells over her shoulder as she walks back through the bar. I run after her, trying to keep up. I look back to thank Honey, but she's already disappeared. "You go to the table, take the drink order, write it on a ticket, then put the ticket here," she points to a silver spike sticking out of the bar. There are papers stacked up. "When your drinks are made, use a tray to carry them to the table. I will put the order ticket on the tray if it's a large order. Got it?"

I nod, trying to replay every word she said.

"Cool, let's go get you a uniform. Everyone settles their bill at the end of the night. Don't let them talk you into saving it for tomorrow." There is a glint of anger in her eyes as she speaks. "If you let them leave without paying their bill, you assume that debt."

She hands me a black leather thing. This might be worse than the camisole.

I try to place the strips of leather deliberately, hoping to get at least some coverage. Staring at myself in the mirror, I take a deep breath. My father would kill me for letting myself get pulled into the situation.

His words of warning echo through my head as I walk down the hallway toward the bar again. "Once you're there, once it has you, The Underworld won't ever let you leave."

I've lived most of my life tucked inside of an apartment, hidden from the lurking evil. Now, in just a few hours, I've found myself consumed by it.

My section is empty most of the time because the tables aren't close enough to the stage. Song after song blares through the speakers. Buttercup, Cookie, Sweetie, Pixie, Candy, Muffin, and several other cutesy food-named women take to the stage.

I'm in awe of what they can do and the way they move their bodies. Mostly, I'm grateful that they are drawing attention from the crowd. No one seems to care about me at all.

That is the only silver lining.

CHAPTER 4

 naïs

HONEY IS ONSTAGE, she's upside down, hanging onto the pole, spinning slowly so that each time she passes the crowd, her widespread legs reveal her.

She has sparkling jewelry between her legs. Not that I meant to look; it's just difficult not to.

There really isn't a safe place to look anywhere in the building. Every dark corner is filled with someone doing something unsavory. I've never felt more lost and out of place in all my life.

"Hey, I haven't seen you here before!" A man grabs my arm, yanking me closer to him.

"Would you like something to drink?" My voice shakes.

His eyes are laser-focused on the thin strip of leather between my legs. "I'm parched, baby." He licks his lips and starts to lean down toward me.

I freeze like a deer in the headlights.

He presses his face into my neck and inhales. I feel the slimy tip of his tongue against my skin. It's the jolt I need to make my body move. Pressing both hands against his chest, I push him away as hard as I can.

It turns out my most impressive physical efforts do very little against a man of this size.

He barely moves, one of his feet sliding back slightly to steady himself against the force of my hands.

A twisted smirk stretches across his face, and my stomach, still queasy from earlier, rolls again. He's liable to hurt me. I can just feel it. I haven't been in contact with many people, but even I, in all of my naïveté, can see that he means me harm.

"P-Please, let me go." I try not to whimper, but it comes out anyway.

He doesn't respond with words, instead walking forward with my arm still tightly in his grip. My body drags, but he might as well be holding nothing.

"Let go!" I ball up the fist of my loose arm and hit him repeatedly.

He looks down at me the way a person looks at a fly. A minor nuisance.

He walks confidently through the club, past the stage. In a dark corner sits a door. Instantly, I know he's leading me there. I drag my feet, trying to dig my heels into the ground. I don't want to go back there. I know nothing good is waiting for me there.

"Come on," he says, tightening his grip and pulling me harder.

"Let me go!" I yell, hoping someone will hear me. There are people everywhere, but no one is paying attention to us. The music is loud, the lights are dim, and there is a dancer on stage. If anyone is seeing this, they don't care to get involved.

His ring-clad hand slaps over my mouth, a sharp pain shooting across my lips as they split under the force of his grip. The metallic taste of blood fills my mouth.

When we reach the door, he opens it and pulls me in with him. It's just like the hallway with the dressing rooms, except the light hanging above us is red.

A sweaty, musty smell hangs in the thick air. Moaning, screaming, and the occasional sound of skin slapping together slip from underneath the doors as we pass by them.

Just as we walk past a door, it opens.

A naked woman with hickies covering her neck and chest steps out. A man is pulling up his pants in the room behind her.

"Is this room free?" The man holding my arm asks her.

"It is now."

Before the other man is even fully dressed, he's pulling me into the room.

My mouth is so dry I can't speak. I look around frantically searching for something, someone, anything.

There is no salvation in this place.

"Yo, who are you? Are you new?" The girl steps back inside the room.

My wide eyes meet hers, and my bloody lips tremble.

"Leto, she's wearing a bar uniform," she says, looking at the man who brought me here. "Sweets, did you agree to come back here with him?"

I shake my head a frantic no, and she reaches forward, grabbing my arm.

"Fuck you, Kitty, mind your own business," he growls at her.

"Leto, you fucking rapist. I swear to God, I'm telling Zion

about this. There is so much willing pussy in this fucking place, and you have to grab the one that isn't offering." She pulls me down the hallway, mumbling to herself, "Mother fucking pig."

Until we're safely on the other side of the door in the club again, I watch the doorframe, waiting for him to step out, but he doesn't. My chest cracks as soon as the door closes, and a loud sob rips through me.

"Oh, geez girl, you alright?" She looks uncomfortable with my crying.

"T-Thank you so much," I sniffle, trying to get a hold of myself.

"Girl, don't even worry about it. Leto should be banned from this place. Where is your dressing room?" I walk in front of her into the other hallway, leading her to the room they gave me. My legs wobble like a baby deer. At this point, I'm beyond caring. I kick the sky-high heels off and carry them the rest of the way.

"Oh shit, you're brand new," she says as she takes in my empty room.

"What was that place?" I ask her as I sit down on the old brown sofa.

"Hon, this is a strip club and brothel. That was the brothel. We affectionately refer to it as Pussy Passage." she laughs. I'm too stunned to laugh.

After a few minutes, she sits down beside me. "Look, I have to go, but come see me tomorrow when you wake up. I'm usually up before noon. My room is the first door on the left; it says 'Kitty,' on my door." She looks at me, studying my face. "My name is Oksana," she almost whispers like it's a secret.

"I'm Anaïs. Um, Babydoll." I'll never get used to that.

She chuckles, "It suits you."

21

"Thank you for helping me."

"Don't mention it," she stands up. "Come find me tomorrow, and I'll show you the ins and outs of this place. I've got to get back to work."

I know I need to go out there again, but I'm so filled with dread and terror. I've only made fifteen dollars. I'm afraid Cinnamon is going to kill me if I hand her a measly dollar and change for the outfit she gave me.

I'm not sure how much of my father's debt I'm going to be able to pay off. It will be a miracle if I last one night here.

CHAPTER 5

 ane

MY FINGERS DRUM over the desk. I'm so bored I may actually die. I hate Gideon. I hate his dopey smile and his stupid hair. He looks like a caricature of a person. An over-exaggerated living personification of every asinine stereotype of a perfect prince charming.

Only he's a dickless fuckwad. Hardly worthy of anyone's swooning glances.

"We just don't know what to do anymore. We could really use your help," Gideon looks at me expectantly.

"I'm going to be honest with you; I zoned out about fifteen minutes back. I have no idea what you're asking for." I can't be bothered to lie. I don't care enough.

He pulls his lips into an irritated line. Zion coughs to cover up a laugh.

"Oh, for fucks sake! Too many people are sneaking across

the border. We need your help!" He raises his voice. At least he cut to the chase this time instead of droning on with some longwinded explanation.

"Lower your voice when you speak to me. I will forgive you for that. Once. I don't suggest you try your luck a second time." I keep my voice flat. I can't let him see my irritation, or he will think he's getting to me.

He looks slightly shaken.

"I don't know what you expect us to do about it. This is hell. Of course, people are trying to escape." I shouldn't have to explain this to him.

"It's a life sentence; they aren't allowed to just leave The Underworld!" The volume of his voice starts to rise again.

"We have a secure border, guards with guns, and dogs. What more do you want from me?" I am so bored. Death, take me now. I drop my head back against my seat and stare up at the ceiling. How many times do we have to have the same fucking conversation?

"Maybe you could send bounty hunters up to find the ones that sneak over?"

Laughter bursts from my chest. Zion cackles loudly beside me. There really is no brain beneath his full head of blonde waves.

"What's so funny?" He folds his arms over his chest.

"You're joking right?" Zion wheezes.

"No." He looks genuinely confused. Poor fool.

"If we send bounty hunters out of The Underworld, you think they would return here? They would step foot over the border and never be seen or heard from again." I explain it to him like he's a child.

"You don't think they would do it for reward money?"

"Leaving hell would be reward enough." Zion wipes the laughter-induced tears from his eyes.

"Well, we need to do something. These are dangerous criminals that are escaping, they can't be allowed to roam freely. You're in charge down here." I don't miss the smug look on his face. "You need to do something about this."

I sigh. This sounds like a lot of work and bullshit that I'm going to have to deal with.

"We might be able to round up a few loyal men that would come back if I sent them. The reward money would have to be substantial though."

He nods, "Money is no object. We need this taken care of. You set the price, and we'll pay it."

"You should hire guards on your side of the fence. Real ones, armed ones. The men you have there now are a joke! Get a group that is willing to blow a hole through anyone trying to sneak across. Part of your problem is that everyone knows that if they can survive the defenses on our side, they'll meet no resistance on your side."

"It's not easy to find people willing to do that, Kane." His voice is curt. The Prince of Sunshine and Butterflies is getting irritated. "Anyone willing to harm others is down here with you!" The look on his face makes me laugh. Does he think that's insulting to me?

"Surely that's untrue. You have plenty of lowlife scum up top, after all, everyone here started there."

Red-faced and furious, he stands from his chair. "I'll reach out when I've discussed the price for bounties." Without another word, he storms out of the room.

"I think you upset him," Zion chuckles, lighting his cigarette.

"Fuck him," I gulp down the last of my now cold coffee.

"Maybe that's precisely what he needs to knock that gigantic stick from his ass. You should hold the next meeting at The Playground."

25

The mere thought makes me laugh. The day he sets foot in a place like that is the day pigs fly. I'm sure he's into some real nasty shit. Those too good to be true, picture-perfect types always are. He would never lower himself to visit our establishments, though; he sees us as lesser than him, he always has.

Dragging myself up, I walk toward the wall of windows, looking out over the sprawling filth that is my kingdom. Dark pollution billows upward from several buildings, blocking out the sun and the color of the sky. A hazy gray-orange covers everything.

My attention is drawn to The Playground by the neon lights that lure my desperate citizens to forget their troubles while creating new ones. It's temporary oblivion. The problems are waiting right outside the door. They merely trade one set of troubles for another.

My mind wanders to the women there. With their practiced smiles and feigned interest. The carnal pleasure that they offer—maybe I should go over there tonight. Maybe the soft touch of a woman, the sweet taste of her tongue—maybe that's what I need.

The world sits in the palm of my hand, every indulgence, every vice, and every desire within reach. I am the master of all. I can do anything I please. I can have anything my heart desires.

That's the problem.

The dead black mass in my chest doesn't desire anything. I am a hollow king.

There is no joy, no excitement, no rush, no meaning. I want to feel something.

I search for meaning in a void, but there is nothing to be found, no spark of life in the endless cycle of hedonism and violence. I am tired—tired of fucking, tired of killing, tired of gambling. The weariness has settled deep into my bones, a dull ache that no amount of distraction can soothe.

Each day drags by, a monotonous crawl toward death. Nothing new ever happens. I wake up, everyone around me cowers and scurries to obey every command, then I go to sleep.

My world is a suffocating loop, and I am trapped in.

"Want to go to The Playground?" Zion smiles at the thought.

Sex, naked women, alcohol, and drugs—none of it has lost its value to him. I can't even remember the last time I was truly pleased by a woman. The touch of skin, a wet, warm pussy, the tight spasm of her orgasm—none of it matters.

I sigh, "sure." It's been a few weeks since my last visit. At the very least, it will be a mild distraction from my growing restlessness.

CHAPTER 6

 naïs

SETTING our shopping bags down on my fold-out sofa bed, I start to pull out some of the outfits we picked.

In the week since my arrival, Oksana has taken me under her wing completely. She's like a big sister that I always wished I had.

After another run-in with a handsy patron at the bar, I've decided to try dancing tonight. The thought of stepping on stage makes my stomach hurt, but I can't handle the bar. Oksana thinks the stage, while terrifying, will actually be a better fit. At least no one can touch me. I dance, then retreat to my dressing room until my next call.

I can't handle another disgusting man putting his hands on me.

We pick through the items.

"I think you should wear this one," she holds out a pretty

pastel purple camisole that has small cloth flowers sewn all over it.

It's my favorite one.

"Look," she turns to me, "I know it's taboo and I'm not supposed to ask, but I have to know because it's driving me crazy. What the fuck did you do to get sent down here?"

"Oh," I chuckle, I've been secretly wanting to ask her the same thing. "I was born here. My dad was convicted and sentenced to life."

"Born here?" Her face is scrunched up, shocked and confused. "What do you mean by born here? Nobody's born here."

"I was born here."

"If you don't want to tell me what you did, I get it." She's looking at me like I'm lying to her.

"I was born here." I repeat.

She just stares at me for a moment, chewing the inside of her lip. "Well, why didn't they send you back up?"

"What do you mean?" I'm completely confused.

"Baby doll, have you ever seen a child here? There are not even schools. There are no kids here. If a baby is born, it is sent back up top. Only people that are convicted live down here. We're here because we've been deemed unsuitable for society. A baby is innocent."

The room spins, and I feel sick. That can't be true.

"That's not possible. My dad, he said, my dad told me…" I choke, the walls closing in around me.

"Wait," she stands up in front of me, "you're telling me your dad was sent down here, did he meet your mom here?"

"No, they were married. When my dad was convicted, my mom came with him."

"Yo, what the fuck?!" She starts pacing around the room, which only makes me more anxious.

"How did they not send you back up when you were born? I don't understand. How did your mom get down here? If she wasn't the one that was convicted, she shouldn't have been able to come! That's not how any of this works! You don't bring your family when they send you down here. It's hell. It's punishment. You don't bring your family like it's some kind of vacation!"

My chest heaves, and I can't breathe. It's like something is wrapping around me, tighter and tighter until I can't fill my lungs at all.

"Hey! Calm down, breathe. We'll figure this out! We can talk to Zion, maybe he will let you speak to his lawyer or something!"

I know she's trying to help, but what she's saying makes everything worse. It feels like the grimy walls of this tiny room are closing in around me.

I gasp and clutch my chest, letting my body slide down to the floor. Tucking my knees into my chest and wrapping my arms around my head, I make myself as small as possible.

I've never been anywhere but here. Before last week, I hadn't even really been outside of our apartment but for a handful of times. I guess it makes sense now. My dad always told me that I had to stay inside because it was too dangerous. While that may have been true, it's starting to become clear that he had another reason.

I feel her in front of me, my vision is blurry when I try to look at her.

"I can't." My whole body shakes, and I feel dizzy.

"It's ok, you're ok. Try to take a breath," she's holding my face in her hands as she kneels in front of me.

I'm trying but I can't. The fear of suffocating makes me panic more. My body thrashes, panicking and struggling in her arms.

"Anaïs," she sits down beside me, pulling me into her arms, "you have to calm down. Think of something that makes you calm. Kittens! Think about kittens!"

I've never seen a kitten in real life, but I learned about different animals online as a child. I think back to the tiny creatures, imagining their adorable faces and how soft they would be to touch.

As I start to breathe normally, she sits beside me, holding me.

"I had a cat when I was a little girl. She was so little. She hated everyone but me. When anyone else was around, she would hide under my bed until they left." She chuckles while petting my hair.

"What was her name?" I sniffle.

"Kimmy."

After several minutes of silence, my breathing is normal, and I feel calmer.

"Want to know how I got down here?"

I nod my head.

"I was sleeping with a very rich politician from up top. A senator. He was married." She's still touching my hair. "I know, I know, it was wrong. He kept telling me how unhappy he was and how he was going to leave his wife for me." She chuckles, "That should've been my first red flag. They never leave the wife."

She sits up and moves her back slightly so that we're facing each other.

"She turns up dead." She's studying my face for my reaction. "They magically have evidence putting me at the scene even though I never went to their house."

I know she wants me to believe her. I can see it in her eyes.

"I put it on everything, Anaïs, I didn't do it. But I didn't

31

have a good attorney. They said I was deranged and jealous. That I wanted him to leave his wife and that I flew into a rage when he broke things off. He didn't, though! He never ended things!"

"Oksana, I believe you." I really do.

"Everyone here says that they're innocent, but I swear to you, I am."

I smile at her. Who am I to judge? I've lived here my whole life!

"Can I help you get ready?" She asks as she stands and then pulls me up to my feet.

"Do we have to?"

She gives me a sympathetic look while laughing, "Yes, we have to. Don't worry, it won't be as bad as you think."

CHAPTER 7

 ane

"KANE!"

Zion shouting my name makes my eyes snap open.

"What the fuck? Are you sleeping?"

I look around the office, for a moment forgetting where I am.

"Fuck. Yeah, I guess I fell asleep." I groan and rub my hands over my face, my eyes burning even in the dim light. The constant insomnia is starting to get to me. I can't focus with the ever-present exhaustion weighing me down.

"Who falls asleep watching strippers?" He sits beside me on the sofa, facing the window overlooking the club.

I knock back the glass of whiskey he put down on the table in front of me.

"Fuck, what is that?" I grimace at the empty glass.

He laughs, "It was Maker's Mark."

This mother fucker.

Lunging forward, I punch him in the stomach. "I told you to stop doing that shit. How many times do you have to give me bottom shelf shit to be satisfied that I can, in fact, taste the difference?"

He's hunched over, clutching his stomach. "Here," he reaches down and hands me a bottle of Dalmore.

Pouring myself a glass, I look out at the woman on the stage. I feel nothing. Well, not nothing; I definitely feel bored.

With a disinterested sigh, I lean back again, closing my eyes. I'm ready for the night to be over. Hell, I'm ready for tomorrow and the next day to be over.

"A brand-new girl is taking the stage tonight. She's something," he chuckles.

"You always say that." I peek one eye open to look at him.

"This time I mean it," he wiggles his eyebrows at me.

He's always so sure that, *insert stupid nickname here*, will be of interest to me. He's wrong every time. Everyone here is only interested in themselves and what I can give them. It's not surprising really, this is The Underworld.

"I'm going to announce her, the guys are really going to lose their shit for this one." He bounces excitedly from his office. His excitement annoys me to no end. How does he still feel happiness and contentment?

Leaning forward I look down at the crowd, studying the men. They are like ravenous dogs, hungry and restless, their gazes locked onto the stage. Two naked dancers move in perfect synchronicity, their bodies a hypnotic dance of sin and allure. The men are captivated—a salivating horde of desperate degenerates.

Their thirst for a woman's touch, for her body, it's palpable. It radiates from their sweat-slicked skin, hangs heavy in the stale, smoky air, and gleams in their eyes. Each man is on the edge of his seat, ready to throw down a large sum of money for a moment of attention from a beautiful woman.

Pathetic.

They don't even attempt to hide it. They track the seductive sway of hips, the arch of a back. The vile thoughts that run through their heads are clear as day. Licking their lips in the dark.

It's like watching a pack of wolves corner a wounded doe. Snarling and vicious, they circle with evil intentions.

This is my kingdom, a cesspool of humanity's darkest urges, a haven for predators. People who would think nothing of making a meal of anyone who keeps even the smallest piece of their soul.

Zion's voice crackles through the microphone, his Cheshire cat grin spreading wide as he teases the crowd. "Tonight, gentlemen, we have something *extra* special for you," he purrs, his words dripping with anticipation. "A new dancer graces our stage this evening, a precious little babydoll making her debut."

The crowd stirs, a collective murmur of excitement rippling through them. They lean forward, eyes glittering with greed, ready to devour whatever innocent lamb Zion is about to throw to the wolves.

He gestures toward the now-empty stage, a spotlight shining on the curtain against the back wall. Like everyone else, I watch, waiting for her to emerge.

The music changes, a slower, haunting melody different from anything I've heard here before. The song is an unusual choice. My interest is piqued.

The lights dim further, casting shadows around the room. A kaleidoscope of colors moves in patterns over the stage.

The darkness, the lights, and the song feel sensual and eerie. It doesn't belong down here.

A voice fills the room, clear and raspy, singing wistfully about finding the strength to stay. It's evocative and ethereal. The words hold meaning beyond the typical erotic subject matter.

The curtain moves, and she steps out into the open.

I'm standing before my brain can catch up to my body. Pressed to the glass, I watch as she walks, barefooted down the stage.

Flowers, flowers everywhere.

She sways, uneasy and unsure about each step and movement. The nervousness on her soft face makes my skin prick. She's afraid. For the first time, possibly ever, the sight of fear is painful to me. She's like a beacon shining in the vast darkness of this place.

The world is gone, there is no ground beneath my feet, no one else here. Just her. My blood boils and churns as I stand unblinking, captivated.

With grace and beauty that is too good for anyone here to witness, she dances. Slow and with poise, she twirls on the stage. A tiny ballerina giving each condemned man a moment of light. Like letting the sunshine into our dark world just long enough to remember what the warmth felt like.

I can't peel my eyes from her.

My heart pounds so forcefully in my chest that it aches. Everything is out of focus and hazy around her.

The flowers on her outfit look like they are spilling out of her chest. They pour out of her, covering her in petals. She reminds me of a flower. Every bit as delicate and small like she could be trampled underfoot.

A little flower in the filth, an angel in hell.

The song ends, and she bows her head down before quickly leaving the stage. Nothing about her routine was sexual or provocative. She never removed a single article of clothing.

I can't make sense of this. I'm affected.

When she steps off stage a darkness settles around my heart, squeezing like a fist. It's worse than the endless void I normally feel. It burns and throbs in my chest. Just a few minutes watching her, and I'm ruined forever. I can't go back to the dark.

Rushing from the room, I push past the crowd that gathered to watch her. I need to find her. Now.

CHAPTER 8

$\mathcal{A}$naïs

WITH MY KNEES STILL SHAKING, I walk back to my dressing room. I wish Oksana was around, but I know she has several dates tonight.

"Babydoll?" Honey knocks on my door, "Can I come in?"

Grateful for a distraction, I quickly open the door for her.

"Holy shit!" Her eyes are wide. "I have never seen the showroom that quiet before!"

My heart sinks. I don't know much about these types of situations, but I thought I did alright. They didn't kick me offstage before the song ended or boo. I saw a bit of money on the stage.

"Everyone was mesmerized!" She's smiling wide, happy.

"Wait? I did alright?"

"Alright? Girl, you crushed it!"

I hardly have time to celebrate when a knock on the door

38

stops us both. I'm shocked the thin piece of plywood is still attached to the hinges after such forceful blows.

When I look to Honey for assurance, she just shrugs.

The man standing behind the door immediately fills me with both fear and calm. The way he looks at me causes goosebumps to swell over my skin.

He doesn't speak, just stands there, staring. I feel heat creeping over my face and chest.

I know who he is almost instantly.

Kane Azrael.

The rumors that buzz through this place about him are somehow accurate and completely off. He is a towering, severe-looking man with a face and body that make you want to sin. It's more than just his looks. There is something in his eyes—something dark and needy—that looks like it could consume me.

"Y-Yes?" I hate how my voice shakes.

He groans and presses his hands to the doorframe.

He's not even trying to hide his gaze, staring openly at my body. The tiny sheer top only hides so much.

"What's your name?" His voice is deep and low. My stomach flutters at the sound. Does he always sound like this? It's carnal and shameless.

"Babydoll-"

"Uh-uh," he stops me, "your real name." If a look could light you on fire, I would be toast. The way he watches me is different from the rest of the men here. It's wanting but not dirty. I'm afraid of him because I know his reputation because everyone knows his preference for violence.

"Anaïs," my throat is dry.

"Anaïs," he whispers with closed eyes.

When his eyes open, a shudder rolls through my spine,

39

causing me to tremble. His tongue peeks out, swiping over his lips.

"Pack your things," there is no room for negotiation in his voice. I'm frozen for a moment, waiting for an explanation that doesn't come.

Tears burn in my eyes, but I ignore them, moving quickly to grab my few possessions. It was only a few hours ago since I carefully organized these items, trying to make this room home. A million thoughts race through my mind. Is he kicking me out? Did he hate the dance so much that he won't allow me to continue here? Where is he taking me?

A thought so terrifying grips my heart that I gasp and drop my belongings.

Is he going to kill me?

Honey and I make eye contact. She's still standing there, obviously uncomfortable, as I scramble around the tiny room. His gaze never leaves me. I don't look at him directly, but I can feel it.

There isn't anything that she can do. Against Kane, everyone is powerless.

Moving as quickly as my shaking nerves will allow, I hope my swift obedience will please him enough to spare my life. My father always taught me to be compliant and immediate if I ever found myself before Kane or his brother.

"This can't be all you have." He looks confused at the three small plastic bags.

"It is." I look down at the floor.

He huffs angrily, looking at the bags.

"Here," he holds open the suit jacket he had draped over his forearm. For a moment we stand in perfect stillness. He's giving me a jacket? His jacket.

"Anaïs," his voice startles me, "put it on."

A soft, clean smell engulfs me as the fabric does. He

reaches forward, pushing one of the sleeves up to grab my wrist. His grip is gentle, holding me with a carefulness that takes me by surprise.

"Come," he walks quickly down the hallway. Looking back at Honey, I mouth a silent goodbye. I have to jog to keep up with his long strides. He must notice my struggling because he slows down slightly. His strides are still longer and faster than mine, but I'm able to keep up now.

As we enter the showroom, a few men notice us, looking away from the girl on the stage. Immediately they turned their eyes, looking anywhere but in our direction.

Zion steps out from behind the bar as we pass it.

"Seriously, Kane," his voice is almost whiney. "Where are you taking her?"

"She's coming with me."

Annoyance covers his face. Standing between the two of them, it's shocking how similar they look. Zion is almost completely covered with tattoos, and Kane doesn't appear to have any, but otherwise, they are nearly identical.

"Just take her up to my office for a while! She is supposed to dance three more times tonight!"

A thought that somehow hadn't occurred to me hits me like a ton of bricks as he speaks. Is that why he's taking me?

His gentle grip tightens, causing me to look up. He's staring at me with rage burning in his eyes. Without a word, he starts walking, his impossibly fast pace from earlier punctuating his anger.

A chauffeur is waiting outside, the back door to a large black SUV already open.

"Take us home, Dec," he nudged me into the car.

"Right away, sir."

I don't miss the way his brows furrowed in confusion.

My mind and my pulse are racing. He's taking me to his house? To rape me and kill me I can only assume.

Plucking up my courage, I peek up at him through my bangs. He's focused on his phone, reading, then typing quickly.

I pick my cuticles inside the sleeves of the jacket so he can't see my fidgeting. I want to look outside, to see the city as we pass through it, but I'm too nervous.

We're driven into a dark underground parking garage. The car rolls to a smooth stop, and before I can blink, the driver is opening the door for us.

"Come," he holds his hand out to me.

I wonder if he can feel it trembling.

I follow him into an elevator. I'm shocked by the cleanliness of everything. The marble floors and smoked mirrors are spotless.

My heart hammers in my throat as we ride up to the top in silence. The quiet wooshing of air and grinding of gears for the elevator's movement are the only sounds.

The doors slide open, and I'm awestruck. Is this his house?

Everything is dark—marble, concrete, and stone in varying shades of gray and black. Floor-to-ceiling windows cover one side of the apartment, the view looks like it stretches on forever.

"You like it," he's not asking.

I nod my head, my mouth still hanging open.

"Good," he nods and walks toward the staircase, stopping after a few steps and turning back to where I'm still standing. "Come."

I nervously follow him up the stairs and down a lonely, dark hallway. The echoing of his shoes tapping against the marble rings loudly in my ears. I am filled with dread every time we approach a door.

He stops in front of a door and pushes it open, waiting for me to look inside.

What horrors await?

I brace myself for the carnage I expect to see. Terror beyond anything my wildest imagination could conjure up. Blood and mutilated bodies, pain, and suffering—the cruelest and most unusual of tortures.

Taking a deep shuddering breath, I step forward.

It's just a bedroom.

CHAPTER 9

 Kane

THE SHOCKED RELIEF on her face is almost comical. I can only guess what her imagination was coming up with.

"This will be your bedroom."

"My bedroom?" Her nose scrunches up. In her confusion, her fear and trepidation have been temporarily forgotten. She looks up at me, her big, round eyes are blue enough to drown in.

"Yes."

I don't say more because I don't know what the fuck I'm doing.

Why did I bring her here? I don't know.

How long will she stay? I don't know.

What is she going to do while she's here? I don't know.

I just couldn't leave her there. The Playground is no place for her.

44

"What is your last name, Anaïs?" I can't just stand here and stare at her all night. I should gather information.

"Poulain."

"I had a few of my shirts brought up, tomorrow a suitable wardrobe will be delivered. If you need anything, I'll be down the hall."

She's still standing in the doorway when I walk down the hallway. If I don't leave now, I will never be able to pull myself away. I have business to attend to.

When I enter my office, I make sure the door stays cracked open so I can hear her if she needs me.

"Anaïs Poulain," I whisper as I type.

No file found.

That's not possible. Everyone has a file.

After trying different spellings and filtering the search down as much as I can, there's still nothing.

She wouldn't lie about her name, would she? I'm not a trusting man by nature, but something about her is believable. Those damn doe eyes.

My fingers drum the desk impatiently as I wait for Zion to answer his phone.

"What?" He must still be pissy that I took his new dancer. He'll have to get over that.

"How did she come to work for you?"

He's hesitating. I feel anger bubbling up in my chest.

"Zion, how the fuck did she start dancing for you?" My anger bubbles up, and I yell into the phone.

He groans, "Her father owed Hanzo almost fifty thousand. His men attempted to rough him up, but apparently they were too rough. They killed him. I bought the debt from Hanzo."

"And you fucking transferred it to her."

My phone cracks in my hand. I'm going to fucking shoot

him. I told him that I would shoot him, and now I'm fucking going to.

Picking up my office phone, I call Declan. I might need some muscle behind this.

"Boss?" He answers on the first ring.

"Dec, I need all the information you can find on the girl, Anaïs Poulain. Start at The Playground and Hanzos. Be quiet about it, I don't want her name floating around."

"Right away, sir."

Dropping the phone I scrub my hands over my face. It's almost three a.m. I wonder if she's asleep.

Walking quietly down the hall, I stop at her door. If she is asleep and I knock, I might wake her. Choosing not to risk it, I silently open the door.

She's in bed, the blanket draped over her body. My jacket is neatly laid across the bench at the end of the bed. Her hair is sprawling across the pillow in long waves. Her lips are slightly parted as she takes soft, shallow breaths. I'm confused by her peacefulness. Confused and maybe a bit jealous.

She sighs in her sleep, a faint, content sound that makes me feel an unsettling calm.

Sitting on one of the armchairs near the end of the bed, I watch her. She's fascinating to me.

Everything about her is small. She looks delicate, break-able. Yet, here she is, fast asleep in the devil's house.

I'm not sure how long I've been here, but I can't seem to pull myself away. The sun is starting to rise in the distance, casting orange light across the ground. The hazy, smokey air outside is cut with the barely visible rays of light that only just signal the change from night to day.

She jerks up, sitting in the bed with wide eyes, staring at me.

Her strawberry blonde hair is a tangled mess as her chest heaves with every breath.

I open my mouth, but before I can speak, my phone rings. It's Declan.

Standing, I answer and walk out of the room.

"Yes."

"Sir, I have a bit of information, but I'm not sure..." He's afraid to tell me.

"Declan," I hate sidestepping, and he knows this. It must be really bad, he doesn't usually show any fear.

"Sorry, Sir. Her father was convicted on forgery charges twenty-one years ago. His wife, Claudie Poulian, was never seen again up top. From what I can gather, sir, she came here with him. It seems Anaïs was born here."

The room spins, and every muscle in my body contracts. She was born here?

"Sir?" He's cautious. "Should I continue?"

"Yes," my voice shakes with the all-encompassing rage that I feel.

"I was able to speak with someone that lived in their apartment building. Several people suspected that he had a child there, but they could never confirm. He kept her in the house until she was older."

"What of her mother?"

"Died a long time ago from what I can gather."

She was born here? If her father wasn't already dead, I would kill him myself. What kind of selfish prick keeps a child here? My throat feels tight like I'm being strangled. What if she wants to go up top? I can't let her leave.

Turning on my heels, I make my way back to her room. I stop outside of her door, taking a few deep breaths to calm my rage before I knock. I hear a small whimper from inside.

"Anaïs?" I push the door open.

47

She's sitting in the middle of the bed, blankets wrapped around her. When I burst through the door, she gasps and scrambles back against the headboard.

"Why are you crying?"

"I just-" she's sniffling and wiping her face frantically, "I can't take it anymore. Why am I here? Are you going to kill me, or-"

"What?" She's barely making sense. All of the sniffling and mumbled words jumble together to make an incomprehensible mess.

She squares her small shoulders and looks me in the eye. "Are you going to kill me?"

"No, I wasn't planning on it."

She blinks a few times, processing my words.

"Then, why am I here?"

"Anaïs, what was the crime that caused you to be sent here?" I ignore her question as I still don't have an answer to it.

Her eyes shift back and forth nervously. She's deciding whether or not to be truthful.

"I was born here." Her voice is so quiet it's difficult to hear her.

I'm pleased with her honesty.

"It's illegal for you to be here without a conviction. You could be sent to the pits."

She gasps and clutches the blankets tightly. "Please, please, I didn't know! My father never told me that I wasn't supposed to be here!"

"You really didn't know?" I look at her, scrutinizing her.

"No, I promise, please, don't send me to the pits!" Fresh tears form in her eyes.

Feigning indifference, I sigh, "I suppose we can sweep it

under the rug, but you can't ever talk about it again. If anyone ever finds out that I showed you leniency-"

"I won't! I'll never mention it again!"

I nod, bile rising in my throat. Without another word, I leave quickly. A horrible feeling lingers in my chest, pressing on my neck. What is this? It's overwhelming and awful. Like a headache behind the eyes. I don't want her to leave. I had to lie to her.

CHAPTER 10

 naïs

AFTER SHOWERING and pulling another one of his soft shirts on, I sit on the bed. I don't know what else to do.

I can't shake the terrible feeling that he's lying to me. He's toying with me. As soon as I get comfortable, he's going to send me to the pits for being here illegally. He is not known for being merciful or for letting things slip.

My father used to tell me stories about the Azrael brothers. Their reputations are known to all, even someone like me, locked away in an apartment for most of my life. I thought the stories were exaggerations, tall tales that grow more and more outlandish as they pass from person to person. The way people looked at him, or rather avoided looking at him, told me what I needed to know. He is as feared as my father said.

He never answered me when I asked why I was here at

his house. I wasn't going to ask again. I don't want to do anything that will anger, displease, or otherwise irritate him.

I rack my brain, searching for any reason why he would want me here.

He must be lulling me into a false sense of security, making me think he means me no harm. It's a sick game to him. It must be. Nothing else makes any sense. I have no money—quite the opposite, in fact. I owe a substantial sum to his brother!

Maybe he has selected me to be a maid in his home?

A knock on the door makes my blood run cold. Any interaction with him leaves me shaken and unsettled.

"Miss Poulain," a soft woman's voice speaks from behind the door.

I run to open it, relieved that it is someone other than Kane. The nervous-looking woman on the other side of the door looks just as surprised to see me as I am to see her.

"I am to..." she hesitates, "do whatever you want to do."

What does that even mean? She must sense my confusion.

"Is there anything you would like to do?" She tries again, "We can shop, or I can give you a tour. Would you like breakfast?"

"Oh, no, thank you. I'm fine to just stay here."

I don't have any money to shop with. I don't want to be in the way.

She looks nervously at her hands. "Are you sure? I've been instructed to take you anywhere you would like to go."

I can't let myself get too comfortable here. I settled in for a long stay at The Playground and look at the way that turned out! It's better that I don't allow myself to feel any sort of security here. That way everything will feel less like a whirlwind upheaval when it changes suddenly.

Sitting on the bed, I scoot as close as I can to the window.

The view is incredible. Not to be mistaken for beautiful. The Underworld is not a place that one might describe as particularly scenic, but there is something about this view.

The sky is gray, thick with hazy pollution that billows up from below. This part of the city is very different from my dad's old apartment. There, every building was made of concrete. Here, most of the highrise buildings are made of mirrored glass that reaches up into the sky.

The dark, murky cool of the air reflects off of the buildings, making everything look like smoke.

I watch as cars drive around on the street below. They're very small from way up here. People walking in the street are even smaller.

Sitting forward on my knees, I press my hands to the glass. Dad always blocked the windows out so I couldn't see out. Watching people is fascinating.

"What are you doing?"

A startled scream rips past my lips as my body jumps. Kane is standing a few steps into the room, watching me.

"I didn't mean to scare you. What are you doing?"

"J-Just looking outside." I pick nervously at my cuticles. I don't want to look at him. He's the devil, but he doesn't have a devil's face. He makes my skin feel hot and my heart beat faster.

"It's so interesting that you didn't want to go out?" He looks confused.

"No. I don't need anyone to take me anywhere. I'm fine to sit here." Safe and out of the way.

"Are you hungry?" His voice dips down into that soft, comforting tone that makes my legs feel wobbly.

"No, thank you."

Uncomfortable silence makes my cheeks burn. For a few

minutes, we stay perfectly still. Every second that passes seems like an eternity.

Looking up at him finally, he's just staring at me. His brows are pulled down, confused, and vexed.

"You want to sit here all day?"

"Yes, that's fine."

"Can I show you the kitchen? That way you can eat when you get hungry?" It's like he's begging.

"Alright," I don't think he's going to leave if I don't agree to something.

I follow just behind him. Every few steps, he turns back to look at me.

I take this opportunity to look at him. He's so tall. He's wearing a black suit. Just like last night. His broad shoulders and back are imposing. Even from behind, it's obvious that there is something exceptional about him. His gait, the way he holds his head, his proud posture. Not just for his mountainous stature and impossibly handsome features, he is extraordinary and terrifying. It's in the air around him.

When we reach the kitchen, he turns, gesturing his hands around.

"You can have anything you like," he's still watching me.

"Thank you," my throat is so dry in his presence.

He's waiting for me to do something. I can feel it.

Stepping forward, I reach into a bowl on the counter, it's full of peaches. I've never had a peach. They don't sell produce in The Underworld. These would have been incredibly expensive to import. Only the very rich can afford luxuries from up top.

It's soft, velvety in my hand.

He's watching me, waiting for me to bite into it. Is he going to kill me if I do? How presumptuous and foolish of me to take something so costly. My fingers tremble. I want to drop it and run.

I peek up at him. His chest is heaving, and his pupils are blown out.

"Take a bite." It's a command, a low growl that makes my stomach clench.

Nervously, I raise the fruit to my lips, taking a small bite. It's thick and sweet in my mouth. The soft, juicy texture and the tangy but delicate taste make my eyes go wide.

I look up at him again, the taste still dancing on my tongue.

"Good," is all he says before walking away quickly with his hands clenched by his sides.

CHAPTER 11

 ane

WHY WON'T she leave the room? It's been three days since she ate the peach in the kitchen. She has declined every invitation to dine with me. As far as I can tell, she's only had a few pieces of toast that she sneaks in the middle of the night.

I don't understand it. As soon as I left her in the kitchen, I called and placed an order for every kind of fruit that was in season up top. Apples, nectarines, apricots, definitely more peaches—everything they have.

She hasn't touched any of it.

My body physically aches at the thought of watching her soft lips as she bites into fruits. The juices wetting her lips. The sweet taste coating her tongue. I should stop thinking about it. I'm sure no one wants to receive a punishment from a man with a raging hard cock standing at full attention in his pants.

55

"Sir?" Declan is standing beside the parked car, holding the door open.

We arrived more quickly than usual today.

Sighing, I slide out of the seat. Another judgment day, another day filled with pathetic scum that beg for mercy they don't deserve. I am not known for my patience, but today I have none.

More than ever, I don't want to be here. Being the ruler of The Underworld has its perks, but this isn't one of them.

How do I get Anaïs out of that room? I sent Declan's girlfriend to offer to show her around or take her shopping. I thought she would like those things. Everything about her is confusing. She doesn't seem to like or want anything.

"Sir?" Declan is obviously trying to keep his facial expression neutral, but his confusion is clear. We're standing in the elevator, the doors are open on the top floor. I have no idea how long we've been here.

Clearing my throat and stepping out, I walk quickly toward the judgment hall. With each step, I find myself growing more enraged.

Why won't she leave that fucking room?

I've not hurt her or so much as raised my voice. I have given her the freedom to move about as she pleases. But she is pleased to sit in that one bedroom endlessly.

"How many today?" I ask as I take my throne.

"Forty, sir," Declan hands me a stack of files.

Ignoring the sniveling group of sniveling criminals, I flip through the files.

Rape, robbery, blackmail, assault with a weapon—the usual suspects. No one ever does anything original.

"You know what?" I turn to the guards standing beside the group, "Fuck it! Death, the lot of them!"

Without waiting for a reply, I leave the room full of wailing and begging.

Declan jogs behind me. "Take me to Zion."

"Right away, sir."

I'm impatient. I need advice. He might not be the most appropriate person to ask, but I don't have anyone else. I need to know how to make her feel more comfortable.

Pushing his bedroom door open, I'm met with the overwhelming smell of sweat, weed smoke, and sex.

Zion is lying in the center of his large bed with a woman on either side of him.

Grabbing a beer from the table, I make my way through the disgusting maze of used condoms and discarded clothes.

"Wake up!" I shout as loudly as possible while pouring the beer over him.

The girls scream and jump out of the bed.

"Yo, what the fuck, Kane?" He grumbles and rolls over, feeling around for the women that are no longer beside him.

"Get out," I point toward the door.

The girls quickly find whatever clothing items they can while trying to make a hasty exit.

"Not cool, man."

"I need your help."

This catches his attention.

"Yeah, what's up?" He sits up, pulling his hair up and tying it back.

"Anaïs won't come out of her room. She isn't really eating. I don't know what to do." I run my hands through my hair. She's so jumpy and afraid. I don't know what else to do.

"Who?" His stupid face scrunches up.

"The girl, stupid mother fucker," I pour the rest of the beer on him.

"Whoa, alright!" He yells and gets up, looking for clothes

on the floor. "I'm just surprised she's still with you. You could have anybody, why do you want some mousy girl that's afraid of her own shadow?"

"You wouldn't understand, and for the record, she's not mousy."

"I mean, I get it, her body—sheesh," he bites into his lip. "She's just so shy."

"Stop talking about her body, or I'll cut your tongue out. Are you going to help me or not?"

He ignores the comment about cutting out his tongue. He rubs his hand over his mouth while he thinks.

"Why don't you take her to the beach house?" He shrugs.

I forgot about the beach house. I don't really have time for vacations. She's never been up top.

"That's actually a good idea." I say more to myself than to him.

"I know it is. Chicks love it there. She'll give up the pussy so fast you won't know what hit you," he smiles fondly at whatever memories he's thinking of.

Lunging forward, I punch him square in the face. Hard enough to bleed, not hard enough to break his nose.

"Ouch! Fucker! That's the last time I help you!"

"I owe you a bullet, jackass, be grateful for the bloody nose."

Sliding back into my seat, I let down the partition. "Dec, have your girlfriend come over. I need her to help Anaïs pack. I'm taking her to the beach house."

This time his attempt at a neutral expression is completely fucked. The shock is very obvious. I know he wants to ask about her but wisely keeps his mouth closed.

"I'll call her right away." He nods his head as I roll up the partition.

A few days at the beach might do us both some good.

CHAPTER 12

 naïs

"ANAÏS?"

I hear my name being called as I quickly try to dry my naked body.

"I, um, one second!" I yell through the door as I rush to wrap the towel around myself.

The girl that never introduces herself but brings me clothing is standing just inside the door. A suitcase sits beside her, and a black shopping bag is in her hand.

"He wants you to pack your things in this suitcase. I brought you this since I never brought you a swimsuit," she smiles.

The packing makes sense. He's ready to boot me back to The Playground. The swimsuit makes less sense. Where will I be swimming?

"A swimsuit?"

59

She looks confused for a moment before realization hits her and her mouth drops open.

"Wait, you don't know where you're going? Oh, God! Maybe it was supposed to be a surprise! Dec didn't tell me!" She's panicking. "Please don't tell him that I told you! Oh my God, he's going to kill me, literally!"

"Whoa, whoa, whoa, calm down! I won't tell anyone anything." I don't want to get her in any trouble.

"Thank you, Anaïs!" She lunges forward, wrapping me in a tight hug.

A throat clearing behind us makes her freeze, her arms still wrapped tightly around my towel-clad body.

"I was just dropping this off. I'll get out of your way!" She runs out of the room.

"I came to see if you're ready to go, I guess not," his eyes move down my body. Everything is warm and jittery. I'm rooted to the ground, watching him openly stare at me.

His eyes move up my legs slowly. I can physically feel his gaze like fingertips grazing my skin. His focus lingers at the top of my thighs for an extra second before continuing upward.

It dawns on me now that he's not wearing a suit. Still all in black, his t-shirt and jeans make him look younger.

I know I shouldn't, but I let my eyes roam over him too. His arms are exposed, tan skin over toned muscle. His skin looks warm and inviting. The memory of his hand on my wrist, of his long, calloused fingers, makes my skin tingle.

Against my better judgment, I look at the front of his pants. My intention was to let my eyes gaze in passing. Only now I can't look away.

The thick, bulging outline pressed against his jeans is equally terrifying and exciting. I feel flushed. What is wrong with me?

I'm afraid, but the fluttering feeling deep in my stomach is outweighing that at the moment. Finally tearing my eyes away, we share a moment of eye contact. It's like looking directly at a bright light. He's powerful and confident, it makes me feel small in his presence.

I should cower in fear, not need to change my panties.

"Get dressed, we will leave in fifteen minutes."

Once I'm alone, my heart slows to a normal pace. I still don't know where he is taking me. Swimming? Maybe he's going to drown me in the Styx.

Where else would we be heading? There are no other bodies of water down here.

The thought of being near that water makes my skin crawl.

Packing quickly, I try not to let my nerves get the better of me. At every turn, he surprises me. I'm starting to get the feeling he truly doesn't mean me harm, but it still doesn't make sense. Does he make a habit of collecting lowly women and setting them up in his house? Not according to the rumors.

Dragging my bag down the hallway toward the stairs, he jogs up to meet me. When he takes the suitcase down for me, I am overwhelmed by confusion to continue.

"Why am I staying here?" I blurt out.

He stops halfway down the stairs, turning toward me, "I want you here."

He seems satisfied with that answer because he turns back and continues walking.

"What? What does that mean? Am I supposed to be a maid? What do you want me to do? I'm just supposed to sleep here? And what about money? I owe a lot of money. How will I earn it?"

He blinks a few times, staring at me like I just spoke in a

language he doesn't understand. My momentary confidence is shattered. What was I thinking? I was basically screaming at him.

"I'm so sorry, I don't know what I was thinking." I clap my hand over my mouth.

"You are not to be a maid," he says, his lips turning slightly upward. This is the closest thing to a smile I've seen from him. Turning and continuing down the stairs, he takes the suitcase. Apparently, that conversation is over, and that is the only contribution he wishes to provide.

I suppose I should feel grateful that he didn't shoot me dead on the spot.

I'm not here to be a maid, but with that answer comes more questions. That was the only logical explanation in my mind for my presence here. I've considered more sinister reasons, dark sexual purposes, but that doesn't feel right.

He scares me, he captivates me, he makes me nervous, and he makes me feel things I don't understand. One thing that he doesn't make me feel is creeped out. His gaze is sometimes curious, sometimes full of lust, but never ominous. He never looks like he wants to hurt me. Devour me maybe, but not hurt.

Declan, his manservant, is waiting with the doors open in the parking garage.

I slide across the cool leather seats, pressing myself as tightly to the window as I can. This back seat is going to feel suffocatingly small when he sits down. I can only hope it's a short ride.

Declan maneuvers the car out of the dark garage into the dingy streets. The hum of the engine a low growl in the stillness. The flickering glow of failing streetlights, casts long shadows across the cracked pavement.

For several minutes, the silence between us is thick,

almost suffocating. My eyes drift to the passing scenery, watching the building whiz past. Soon, an acrid stench begins to seep into the car. The Styx— slimy green water that looks more like toxic sludge. You can always smell it before you see it.

"Where are we going?" The words finally push past the knot in my throat.

"My beach house."

I love that he answers things in as few words as possible. It really has a way of easing my mind and making me feel informed! He never offers even a single word more than he has to.

"Beach house?"

"Yeah, up top." He's so casual.

I gasp loudly, and my spine jolts pin straight. We're going up top? It takes all of my self-control not to press my nose to the glass. I want to see everything.

CHAPTER 13

 ane

SHE'S EXCITED. I may not understand most things about her but I can see that she is excited.

"How long does it take to get there?" She's almost bouncing in the seat.

"A few hours."

"I thought no one could leave?" She looks back at me, a confused crease forming between her brows.

"I can and you are my guest." And there is no file indicating that you belong down here so you are not bound here either but I won't mention that.

The river Styx sloshes and swirls beside the road, all of its putrid green bacteria-filled waves lapping at the shore. The car maneuvers onto the bridge. She is pressed to the glass, looking at the scum below.

We pass a bus driving in the opposite direction. For a

moment as we line up perfectly side by side, the wails and screams of the passengers can be heard. Her back tenses and she looks at me, fear in her sparkling eyes.

"Prepare yourself. When we reach the border, it will be worse."

She gulps and sits back against her seat, her small fingers twisting in her lap. The curiosity and eagerness disappeared from her face.

The high wall of the border appears on the horizon, small and unimposing. At this distance, it doesn't look like a place where people are dragged from the world above to spend the rest of their natural lives here. It is a place of misery, of shrieking cries, and desperation. The people there are being ripped away from their lives to start anew in hell.

The horrors of this place are whispered behind closed doors but they don't really know. In some ways, it's just like it is up top. Everyone is playing a role. Behaving and showing the world a righteous and morally sound person. Here, it's the opposite. Everyone, regardless of their crimes, exhibits their darkest side. Show your deepest, most deprived parts.

I normally relish bad behavior. The leader of the Underworld is obviously not opposed to a bit of rule-breaking. The irony of my attraction to the sweet woman sitting beside me is not lost on me.

The closer we get to the border crossing, the more my irritation grows. It's going to upset her. The thought of her in distress makes me irrationally angry. This trip is for her, to make her happy.

"Stop the car," I bark angrily at Declan before the partition has time to fully open.

He pulls over immediately, his eyes watching me in the rearview mirror.

Anaïs is watching me too. I can feel her gaze.

Sliding out of the car, I walk a few steps away. Declan was surprised and didn't get out fast enough to open the door for me. I hear his door open and quickly close as he gets out of the car.

Pulling out my phone I dial Chief Marely, the head agent at the border crossing.

"Sir," he sounds nervous already.

"Marley, I need you to shut down the inbound lanes to all traffic until you hear from me."

"I, well, Mr. Azrael, that will be practically-"

"Don't give me fucking excuses Marley. Get it done right now. I'll be crossing through the outbound side in ten minutes. When I come through I want to hear silence. Back all the traffic up to where the road divides at the tunnels. You have ten minutes."

I can hear him panicking before the line goes dead.

Walking back toward the car, Declan makes sure to get the door this time.

"Is everything alright?" She looks nervous as I reenter the backseat.

"Yes, everything will be fine."

She's picking at her fingers again. She does it whenever she's anxious. Without thinking I reach out, taking her hand in mine. She gasps obviously surprised but doesn't pull away. Her hand is so soft and small in mine.

As Dec brings us closer to the border, everyone is tense. She fidgets in her seat, her hand tightening slightly around mine. The closer we get to the large guarded dividers the straighter she sits in her seat. Her eyes are glued to the heavily armed men as we pass.

With a locked jaw, I listen, straining to hear the miserable sounds of the buses on the other side of the cement dividers. As we enter the tunnel I breathe a sigh of relief.

I can't see her as we move through the darkness, but I can feel her. The nervous excitement is there in every squeeze of her hands and tap of her foot.

The light from the end of the tunnel can finally be seen. Her breath is shaky and quick.

"Are you alright?"

"Is it stupid that I'm nervous?"

"No." She is incapable of stupidity.

The tunnel opens up to blue skies as we drive onto the treelined highway.

She gasps and looks at me, a shining smile on her face and tears in her eyes. She is brighter than the sun. The world that is whizzing past the window can't hold a candle to her. I don't even care to look. The sky is blue and the sun is shining but she has bewitched me.

The lush greenery has all of her attention. We don't have plants or things that grow in The Underworld.

> Open the inbound lanes.

I send him a quick text, not wanting to tear my eyes away from her. The awestruck wonder on her face stirs something in me that I've never felt before. A churning, gnawing excitement burns in my veins. It's as if I am seeing everything for the first time, watching her.

"Kane," she whispers, and my body jerks slightly. I've never heard her speak my name. Soft and sweet, in her voice that both soothes me and sets me ablaze.

I want to hear it again and again. It takes all of my self control to keep from asking her to repeat it now.

"It's so beautiful. Look at the trees," she looks back at me, "look how tall they are! Everything is so green. I never knew how green it would be…"

"Look over here," I point toward my window. The mountains open into a wide valley with a river rushing through the center. She inches closer to me, our legs touching as she tries to get a clearer view.

She is all that is good and pure and lovely.

Tears pool in her eyes and her lips part as she stares, completely astonished, at the world around us. I never cared about any of it before but right here, watching her, I get it.

A tingle at the base of my skull moves through my limbs like fire in my veins, spreading rapidly, untamed and hellbent on destruction. Like a flash of bright light everything is illuminated and crystal clear.

She will be the queen in hell.

CHAPTER 14

 naïs

IT'S SO beautiful I can't stop crying. The sky is so clear and blue it doesn't feel real. I've seen pictures of the sky, of the ocean, and forests full of trees. Nothing beats seeing it with my own eyes.

The wide valley below us is so breathtaking I can hardly believe it's real. This world is opposite to where we come from in every sense of the word.

Where this is light and beauty, we live in grim darkness. The warmth from the sun beats down so strongly that I can feel it on my skin.

"Do you like it?" Kane's voice startles me.

"I can't believe this exists."

"Just wait until we get to the ocean."

Something about him feels different. He's different. I can't quite put my finger on it. He seems looser, less angry, and serious. The jeans and shirt, the relaxed way he's sitting, the calm in his voice. He's always handsome, devilishly so, with a cool, enigmatic confidence about him that draws me in. Now, he's lighter. The nervousness I often feel about doing or saying the wrong thing is gone. The skittish energy that is coursing through me is a result of being so close to him, at his leg touching mine, at the feeling of his eyes on me.

"You're staring." There is amusement in his voice that keeps me from blushing too severely at being caught watching him.

"You're—" right. He's completely right.

"Don't be embarrassed; you can stare at me. I stare at you too."

His words catch me off guard.

As I feared from the start, I am beginning to feel the vigilant anxiety that kept me quiet and safe starting to slip away. His even temper and kindness have made me feel too comfortable. That in and of itself is dangerous. I'm going to make a mistake. I'm going to say something that will anger him.

"Are you hungry?" His low voice cuts through my inner panic at not feeling enough panic in his presence.

"Umm." I am, I always am.

"Here," he reaches into a black bag on the floor. Handing me a glass container. I can see before pulling it open that there are cut fruits inside of it.

Oh God, not fruits again. My mouth starts to water just thinking about it.

"Go ahead," he sounds almost eager.

Picking up one of the slices of fruit, maybe an apple? I bring it to my lips. If I wasn't sure before, I am now. His sharp intake of breath and slight movement forward confirm that he's watching in anticipation.

Taking a small bite, my eyes flutter involuntarily. Sweet, tangy, soft but still firm.

"Is this apple?"

"Nectarine," his voice makes my stomach muscles clench.

"Would you like a piece?" I offer him the bowl.

Big mistake. Huge.

He takes a piece, his eyes never leaving mine. It moves between his fingers before he takes it up to his lips. I watch with rapture as he bites into the sweet fruit. His perfect teeth and soft lips make me feel shaky. Anything he chooses to do becomes the new sexiest thing I've ever seen.

Forcing my gaze away from his mouth, I look out the window as we approach a bridge. I've never seen so much water before. This place makes the Styx look small.

As the car moves away from the ground, I'm glued to the window again. The blue water, the treelined shores, the sky —it's too good to be true. Everything is too perfect to be real.

"When was the last time you came up top?" I can't believe he doesn't spend more time here. If I was allowed to leave, I would never go back.

"It's been a few years."

My face must show my shock because his mouth moves again, turning slightly upward.

"I'm a very busy man, The Underworld doesn't run itself."

"Right, of course." I feel strangely sad as the car comes to the other side of the bridge. What a strange feeling to be so high in the air, suspended over the water. It felt free, like flying.

Leaning against my window I start to feel myself getting drowsy. I've never been in the car for so long. The vibrations and gentle rocking are making it hard to keep my eyes open even with my excitement.

A warm, low thumping keeps rhythm in my dreams. It's slow but steady, like a bass drum.

"Anaïs," his voice is quiet. "Wake up, we're almost there."

My eyes flutter open. My head is against his chest, his heartbeat thumping in my ears. My cheeks burn, and I force my gaze down. My hand is on his lap, resting high on his thigh. The burn on my face goes from a slight tingle to a five-alarm fire. Moving slowly, trying to avoid detection, I slide my hand away from his lap.

"Look," he's pointing out the window.

On the horizon, the orange sky meets with a never ending blue expanse. The ocean. The setting sun looks like it's going to drop right into the water.

"We're almost to the house, I didn't want you to sleep through the last part of the drive." I feel him behind me, resting his hand on my shoulder. It's comforting. Being up top, and seeing the ocean, it's dizzying. His hand feels like it's holding me to the ground, keeping me from floating away.

"Here," he reaches around me, pushing a button that brings the window down into the door. The warm air and salty smell wash over me. A giggle bubbles up in my throat. If this is all a trick, if he is building me up only to crush me later, this moment will make it worth it.

Whatever happens in the future, no matter what comes, this moment will settle into my brain. Nothing will ever be the same.

"Why are you laughing?"

The orange glow is all over him, radiant and even more striking than normal.

"Thank you for bringing me here."

His fingers softly move through my hair, delicately moving the strands off of my shoulder. He doesn't speak, but he doesn't need to. There is nothing uncomfortable about the silence.

"I wish the sun didn't have to set."

"Why?" His voice is so soft that if I weren't sitting beside him, looking right at him, I wouldn't believe it was him at all.

"This was the perfect day."

His mouth pulls into a line. I think he's upset. "Tomorrow will be better, I promise you."

CHAPTER 15

 naïs

MAKING my way toward the curtains in the dark is tricky. I don't know the layout of this room yet. I'm too excited to sleep. I'm sure the sun hasn't risen yet. I want to watch from my window if I can ever get to it.

Using the wall as my guide, I take careful steps in what I hope is the right direction.

My foot kicks something before the rest of my body feels it. Stepping to the side with my other foot, I try to keep my balance, but whatever it is, my other foot hits it too. In the darkness, my mind can't comprehend what it could possibly be, a chair isn't shaped like that.

A grunt in the dark makes me scream as I fall back to the floor.

"Anaïs," it's Kane. His voice is thick and tired but alert.

A clicking sound, then the overhead light illuminates the room.

"Kane!" I'm breathless and surprised.

In front of me is Kane seated in an armchair with his legs stretched out in front of him. I would have fallen whether he was here or not. The question remains, why is he here?

"What are you doing in here?"

He clears his throat and sits up. Was he sleeping?

Instead of speaking, he looks around, his eyes moving over the floor like he's in deep concentration.

"I promised today would be better, get dressed. A swimsuit..." He stands abruptly and clears his throat, "Come downstairs when you're ready."

He never answered my question. He does that a lot.

I know that he's waiting, but I continue toward the window. When the thick, dark curtain is drawn back, I gasp. The sky is light, pink hues streaking across the early morning blue. My room is at the top of the house, on the fourth floor. Water stretches out in front of me as far as the eye can see.

For a moment, I can't tear myself away. I feel a deep, heavy longing in my heart. Thinking about places like this was a nice dream, a distraction from the sadness and filth. The experience of being here is like bursting a bubble. It's not a fantasy, it's a real place. If not for Kane, I never would have been allowed to see it. It's here, and it's real, but it's out of reach.

A man is walking on the sand, a fluffy white dog scurrying around his feet. I watch the little animal play freely. It darts across the sand, running into the shallow surf before running quickly back to the man. Over and over again, it runs to the edge of the water. The sadness lifts the longer I watch.

Realization hits me, I don't know how long I've been standing here.

The swimsuit sits on the top of my suitcase. Taunting me. Staring at me.

I've never worn a swimsuit before, and this one is particularly small. It looks strikingly similar to the small pieces of fabric Honey had offered me at The Playground. Pulling the deep green fabric up my legs, I try to adjust it to cover, well, any part of me. Turning to the mirror, my eyes widen at my fully exposed backside. The tiny strip of fabric in the front does almost nothing to cover the front of me either.

Tying the matching top over my chest, I sigh, at least they're covered. Pulling on a lacy-looking robe that was also in the bag with the swimsuit and a large floppy hat, I leave the room. I'm flustered and nervous.

Walking slowly, I distract myself by looking around the house. It is light and airy, mostly white with windows everywhere. It's diametrically opposite to his home in The Underworld.

"There you are," Kane's voice at the bottom of the stairs startles me.

He is wearing black shorts. Only black shorts.

My eyes move rapidly over him, unable to make a decision on where to look. His eyes appear to be doing the same, roaming unabashedly over my body. His chest, his arms, his smooth, tan skin—everything about him is alluring.

I feel warm, like the temperature has gone up several degrees. His eyes move slowly, taking in every detail. His eyes touch me physically, like sweeping fingertips brushing my skin. Goosebumps spread everywhere.

We stand frozen, both of us staring at the other.

"Come," he turns on his heels, pulling himself away.

I follow him into the kitchen, where trays of food are set out on the bar.

"Did you cook this?" I gape at the spread.

"No, my chef did."

Chef? I look around the kitchen, but we're alone.

He pulls a high bar stool out for me to sit on. My mouth waters as I look at the food. I've only eaten small things that I can sneak quickly in the middle of the night.

"Eat," he sets a plate in front of me as he sits in the seat next to mine.

Starting small, I take fruit and a waffle. After only a few bites, my shyness fades, and I start eating larger bites more quickly. Everything is delicious.

"I knew you were hungry." His voice is soft, but his face looks stern, angry. "You need to eat Anaïs, everything is available to you. If you want it, eat it. If you desire something I don't have, I will get it for you. Don't sneak toast in the middle of the night anymore. Eat."

I nearly choke. He knows about my sneaky toast?

"I... alright, I'll eat." I pick at my cuticles.

"Are you ready? I want to show you something."

Excitement makes my steps bouncy as I follow him out the large glass doors out toward the sand. With a hesitating step, I put my foot down into the floury powder. When my eyes shoot up to find Kane, he's standing a few steps ahead of me, watching me.

"It's so weird," I wiggle my toes.

His lips pull upward into something unexpected and beautiful. A genuine smile.

CHAPTER 16

 ane

WHAT SHOULD HAVE BEEN a five-minute stroll down the beach took twenty-five minutes. She keeps stopping to look at things or to pick up shiny, smooth rocks and seashells.

Her eyes are as bright as the sun that shines down on her red-tinted blonde hair. The lust I felt seeing her sinful body has melted into something else, something soft and protective. She is unexpectedly good, like sugar on my tongue. I want to preserve her like a flower in winter, to keep the frost from her petals and prolong the bloom.

"What is this?" She asks, squinting up at me. We've finally reached the large rocks.

"Tidepools."

"Will there be things in there? Living things?" She takes several curious steps forward.

"Yes, it was high tide last night, there should be."

78

She's climbing into the rocks before my sentence is complete.

"Step carefully, don't cut your feet." I follow after her, holding her arm to make sure she doesn't slip.

She looks down at the shallow pools of water in the rocks and then back up at me.

The next hour passes in a whirlwind of exploration. She leaves no area unsearched. Starfish, seashells, barnacles, urchins, she finds them all. Carefully studying them before moving on to the next.

I've never been as excited about anything in my life as she is about an anemone.

"Kane?" her soft hand sliding into mine so I can help her down into the sand from the rocks.

"Yes?"

"Can we... Do you want to get in the water?" She seems embarrassed to ask.

"Do you want to get in?"

"Yes."

Still holding her hand, I walk across the sand to the water lapping at the shore. The cold makes her squeal slightly, but she presses forward, knee-deep, hips, then just under the swell of her breasts.

A group of young women yell and shout, playing in the water a ways down the beach. She watches them, pausing to observe their playful shouts and splashes. There is something far away and sad in her eyes.

When she looks away, back at me, she smiles, but it's sad; it doesn't make her eyes crinkle in the corners like a real smile.

"Would you like me to make them leave?"

"What?" She looks surprised, then she laughs.

Now I'm completely confused.

"Are they bothering you?"

"No!" she's still laughing. "Plus, we can't just make people leave the beach."

She forgets who I am. I can make anyone do anything, even up top. I only need mention dragging them back down to hell with me, and they would scurry away quickly.

"It's just that it would be nice to have a friend." Her voice is small.

"I'm your friend."

A shocked laugh bubbles up from her chest. With wide eyes, she slaps her hand over her mouth to physically stop the laughter.

"Why do you laugh? You don't consider me a friend?"

"We don't know anything about each other!" Her hand drops down to her hip.

"What do you want to know?"

"Frankly, anything. Everything?" She looks unsure of herself. She's still very cautious around me.

"For everything, I tell you, I want to know something about you as well."

She nods.

Favorite color, food, song, or book. I learned that she was taught at home by her father and had an affinity for arithmetic.

"What is your biggest fear?" She asks as we walk along the water, the house a tiny speck far in the distance.

"I'm not afraid of anything."

She stops mid-step and grabs my arm, "That can't be true!"

"Anaïs, I rule The Underworld. What could possibly scare me? What is your biggest fear?"

"I'm afraid of everything! The rats at home are probably top of the list."

I know she's joking, but I'm so caught off guard. The laughter that bursts from my chest feels foreign.

"They're very large, aren't they?" She laughs beside me.

When we start to walk again, her shoulder bumps mine. Every time she nudges me, a thrilling shiver runs down my spine.

"That night at The Playground, why did you choose that song?" I've been wondering about this since then.

"Oksana asked the same question," she looks suddenly thoughtful, "I just think it's beautiful. There is something about it that's haunting, but in a good way."

I agree.

"Who is Oksana?"

Her face falls, sadness taking over her delicate features. "My friend. She took care of me and taught me how to survive there when I was new and terrified."

"You miss her?"

"I do. She protected me."

I open my mouth to speak when a large wave crashes to the shore, sending a swiftly rolling rush of water toward us. Hand in hand, we run up the beach, trying to avoid being knocked over.

She looks happy and free.

At the sight of her smiling face, I am overcome.

Pulling her toward me by the hand, I press my lips to hers. For a moment she is perfectly still, her heart hammering in her chest. When her lips move with mine, a deep, satisfied shudder runs down my spine.

She is delicious. Honey on my tongue.

Her body melts into mine. I know she's shy, so I need to be careful with how far I take this. I can't control my cock though.

I'm aggressively hard against her stomach. A tiny whimper, a soft hum, a nearly undetectable moan—the sighs that pass her lips.

Her eyelids flutter. Her fingers grip my arms tightly. Her body presses forward, more of her warm skin on mine. Skin that tastes faintly of salt but mostly like her.

The thought of touching her - fuck. My fingers itch, desperate to reach down and slide into her almost nonexistent bikini bottoms.

A groan vibrates in my chest. I want to touch her pussy. To lick it. To spread her open.

Her body trembles against mine, our mouths still exploring, massaging, and tasting. I can see it, in pornographic detail, my cock disappearing between her legs.

My hands move from her waist to her hips, then from her hips to her ass. I can't stop them.

I'm about to burst into flames.

Moving one of my hands slowly, I slide past the hem of her tiny bikini. She tenses and pulls back enough to look at me with wide-eyed shock.

My fingers push lower until they are parting her soft lips. Slick, hot wetness coats my fingers. Her whole body is tense, with knotted muscles that tremble under my hands.

If I don't stop myself, I'm going to fuck her here, on the sand, for all to see.

My fingers press further, to the tight little bud at the top of her sex. When I circle my finger over it she lets out a tiny sound, a whimpering moan. My blood churns. I'm blinded to anything beyond her, beyond the delicate, wet flesh of her perfect, tight cunt.

Somewhere down the beach, a shrieking laugh breaks the trance, and I pull my hand away from her. What the fuck am I doing? I've never been like this—out of control, hormonal.

We stand in silence for a moment, she teeters on her feet.

I can't get a read on her, is she relieved or upset? Taking her hand, I walk her back toward the house.

Her shoulders are slumped down, defeated, or maybe disgusted? I don't know.

Fuck.

When we get to the house, I take her to her floor and then practically sprint to my room. She looks like she wants to say something, but she never does.

CHAPTER 17

 naïs

WHAT JUST HAPPENED?

When he grabbed me and kissed me, I thought I was hallucinating it. Why would *he* want to kiss *me*?

His mouth was so... everything. It was so intense and tingly. Touching his skin, his hands on me, it felt so good. So perfect. He is so tall, like a fortress that surrounds me. I wanted desperately to run my fingers through his dark tousled hair.

I didn't even know I wanted him to kiss me until he did it. The thought had never really occurred to me. Because... why would it?

Kane Azrael. King in hell. Ruler of The Underworld kissed me. Me! My body hums at the memory.

It started out slow, just soft lips touching with gentle pressure. It grew, rapidly changing into a hot, heavy, groping, licking, sucking kiss. His mouth was everywhere. His tongue. Oh God, his tongue. It's so soft and wet. He swept it over my lips and brushed it over my tongue.

Standing under the hot spray of the shower, I'm still trying to piece together what happened. He kissed me, and it felt incredible but also frightening.

Then he put his hand between my legs.

I know about anatomy, reproduction, and sex. I just wasn't expecting it to feel like that. I spent a week at The Playground, I've seen all manner of sexual activity. Nothing I ever witnessed seemed like this. At The Playground, most of the women were moaning loudly and saying things like, "Yes, daddy," and "You're so hard for me, handsome," but they looked dead behind their eyes.

This was not that.

I felt very much alive. Alive and burning up.

It felt like my heart was hammering between my legs. My body felt soft and fluttery, like my bones were too mushy to keep me upright.

The feeling of his hands on me, the wet, hot, achy feeling between my legs, his hard body. Heat runs through my body, pooling in my abdomen.

Turning off the faucet, I grab my robe and rush out of my room. I know he's on the floor below mine. In a moment of uncharacteristic bravery and possibly incredible stupidity, I march toward the stairs. I blame my scrambled brain.

I wanted to say something, to tell him that his touch was welcome. I didn't know what to say or how to say it. Then he was gone.

The door is cracked open, but he doesn't respond when I knock.

"Kane?" I creep into the room like I'm there to steal something.

His room is dark, the thick curtains are still drawn, blocking out the sunlight. I'm not surprised by this. Dark and moody, brooding—it's kind of his aesthetic.

A stream of light from the cracked open bathroom door is like a beacon drawing me in. I shouldn't be here. I should leave. My feet step forward anyway.

"Kane?" The shower is running. I'm sure he can't hear my trembling whisper.

Peeking into the bathroom, the steamy, thick air is suffocating, but that's not what stops my breath short.

Inside the glass shower, he's standing under the cascading water, one arm up, supporting his weight against the tiled wall. A low groan hits me like an electric poker straight to the stomach.

With a gasp, I step back, colliding with the wall beside the door. He looks up. I brace myself against the wall, waiting for him to yell, to scream, to jump out and punish me.

He doesn't, though.

He just looks at me, watching me. His fist is wrapped around his length, stroking up and down slowly. Each pump of his hand makes my stomach clench.

His eyes pinch closed, and a sound, like a growl and a groan, slips through his parted lips.

My gaze wanders down his wet chest, over his stomach, and down to his hand again.

Oh, God.

Peeking back up at his face, his eyes are open again, staring right at me. His chest starts to heave, rising and falling faster and faster.

I know I should look away, I should leave the room, but I can't.

I want to step forward and look more closely at him. He looks very large and thick, even in his own hand.

The bulges tenting the pants of the men at The Playground did not look like this. I wonder what it would feel like in my hand. The skin looks soft. I wonder what it would feel like pressing where his fingers had been earlier.

I wish he would let go so I could see it fully.

"Fuck," he groans as he drops his head back. His Adams apple bobs as he swallows. I find myself swallowing too, my body mimicking the action. Why am I breathing so hard?

I have to squeeze my thighs together to try to ease the ache that is building by the second.

His jaw drops open, and a loud moan vibrates straight to my soaking wet core. His eyes never leave mine as his chest jerks sharply.

He pants my name as he twitches, thick white streams of fluid spurting out of him. I can't look away. Each jerk has a corresponding pulsating throb in my stomach. Hearing my name leave his lips with so much pleasure on his face makes my knees wobble. I'm grateful for the wall behind me, I would fall without it.

Dropping his hand, he looks up, letting the water run over his face. When he steps out from behind the glass, he wraps a towel low on his hips, letting water drip on the tiles as he stalks toward me.

I'm in desperate need of water, my throat has never been so dry. The tiny droplets rolling down his chest tempt me.

I shake the absurd thought from my head. One kiss and I've forgotten every survival instinct I have. He might have initiated a kiss, but I need to be careful here.

Oksana told me all about Zion's "flavor of the week" attitude with women. She warned me that if he wanted me, I shouldn't expect any lasting favor. I can only assume Kane is as fickle as his younger brother.

Again with the false sense of security.

87

"Come," he reaches down and takes my hand.

"W-Where are we going?" My nervousness and the thrill of adrenaline course through me making me tremble everywhere.

"To bed." There is a slight hint of amusement in his voice.

My knees almost give out as my imagination runs wild with ideas about what he could mean by that.

"Would you like sleep or pleasure?" He's so calm.

Warning! Danger Ahead! Proceed with caution!

Alarm bells are ringing off in my head. I consider that this might be a once-in-a-lifetime opportunity. A chance to lay beneath this man doesn't come around every day.

My father's disapproving face flashes in my mind. He would be so angry at me for even entertaining the thought.

"S-Sleep," my voice is hoarse and completely full of doubt.

His lips turn slightly upward, and he pulls me the rest of the distance to the bed. He lies down and immediately closes his eyes.

With slow hesitation, I climb into the silky black sheets and pull the blanket up to my neck.

This is fine. Just close your eyes and sleep. Everything is fine.

Peeking my eyes open I try to look at him without making any movement. His eyes are open, and he's looking at me.

Snapping my eyes closed, he chuckles. The sound ignites the same thumping pressure between my legs.

This is going to be a very long night.

CHAPTER 18

 ane

I KNOW she's still awake. She's trying to pretend that she's sleeping, but I watch her sleep. This is not how she breathes when she sleeps.

"Anaïs?"

She hesitates to answer, still holding onto the charade of being asleep.

"Yes?" Her voice is small, squeaky.

"Can't sleep?"

"No, not yet." There is a tremble in her voice that makes my body buzz.

"Can I help you?"

"How?" I'm sure if she was facing me, I would find her brow furrowed.

"You're too tense, let me help you relax." So many ideas float around in my head.

"How?" She questions everything, but she's curious and not upset.

My mouth waters at the possibilities. "I would love to eat your pussy."

She gasps, her head jerking up to look at me. With one swift rolling motion, I'm on my side next to her.

"You want to—" She's blushing all the way down her chest.

"May I?" I take the bottom of her robe between my fingers.

She gulps, wide-eyed and nervous, but there is something else there too. She's excited. She's going to let me.

The smallest nod, and I spring into action. Spreading her robe to the side, I'm surprised to find her naked underneath.

Taking her thighs in my hands, I gently pry them open.

"Holy fucking shit." The words practically choke me. I knew it. Soft and pink and fucking soaked.

I've never been hungrier than I am right now.

I lose track of time, sitting between her spread open legs, memorizing every tiny detail. Fuck the ocean, sunsets, and pretty flowers that grow up top. There is nothing beyond this, the opening between her legs.

It's a portal between worlds, where life begins—the most beautiful things I've ever seen.

If I'm given the choice, at the hour of my death, I would like to be right here.

Dragging the tips of my fingers through the tender, swollen flesh, I feel the burning, the ache, the telltale pressure on my spine. Simply touching her is enough to undo me.

"You're so beautiful." I'm struck stupid and unable to articulate the thoughts spinning through my head.

Her body jerks involuntarily at each stroke of my fingers.

She's squirming and wiggling, unable to keep still as her desperation grows. My own desperation is at an all-time high. I'm lightheaded. All of my blood has pooled in my cock.

Bringing my face down closer, I feel her body tense. Inhaling a deep breath, drinking in her smell, my eyes flutter closed as my tongue finally makes contact with her skin. The subtly sweet taste of her draws a moan from deep inside me.

If I thought I was painfully hard before, I had no idea how agonizing it could get. Each swipe of my tongue makes my cock throb and leak.

"Oh my... *God,*" she moans, her legs shaking.

When I suck her clit her legs snap closed around my head, her thighs holding me there.

"K-Kane," her voice is shaky but loud, not timid or mumbling anymore. Hearing her say my name is always something I relish, she says it so rarely I treasure it. Hearing her moan it? My self-control is starting to slip.

With a pattern of long, sweeping licks, small strokes, and sucking, I work her clit until she starts to tremble and shake. Then I press one finger into her.

"*Fuuuck,*" I have to close my eyes and take a breath. She's so wet. The warmth and suffocating tightness around my finger make my cock twitch. I can't even imagine what it would feel like to be inside of her. The pressure alone will probably kill me.

My hips thrust forward against the mattress, it's not enough, it does nothing to ease the ache. I want to stretch her, to feel that tightness over my cock, to sink into the depths of her womb.

Curling one finger, her walls tighten around me, and she cries out. Adding a beckoning finger motion to the pattern with my tongue has her body writhing, rolling on the bed.

Rapid panting breaths, moans, whimpers, pleasure-filled sighs, every sound she makes brings me closer to the edge.

"Kane!" Her body shudders, and she arches upward, pushing herself against my mouth forcefully. I continue my assault on her senses, moving my finger faster inside of her. She's close; I can feel it in the way her thighs tremble around my head.

"Yes!" It's a broken cry, a half-scream cut off by a loud moan as her body finally yields to my touch. I slurp and suck against her pulsating pussy. Not a single drop of this will go to waste. Her hand flies down and grips my hair tight, right at the root.

I'm so surprised by the slight sting in my scalp that I rut my hips forward into the mattress. I need to fuck her. I'll go insane if I don't. I'm consumed, feeling nothing beyond the churning in my blood.

When she releases my hair, I slide back, the towel around my hips falling open.

My cock stands upright, red and angry with precum dripping down the sides. I'm so swollen and sensitive that the air chafes.

Her satiated face turns to one of panic.

"Anaïs," I don't recognize my own voice. For the first time in my life, I feel powerless. Literally on my knees before her. I'm begging.

She keeps looking between my face and my cock. Fear growing in her eyes with each pass.

"Kane," the shakiness in her voice tells me all I need to know.

She's not ready.

Taking my raging cock in my fist, I hiss as the sensitive skin adjusts.

Staring down at her perfectly pink, glistening pussy I start to pump my hand.

"Close your eyes. I won't do anything to you," I barely choke out.

Her eyes flutter closed, and I lean down over her, holding my body up with my knees and arm. I won't let myself touch her, I don't think I can take it, but at least I'm between her legs.

She wiggles but doesn't open her eyes. Even in this state of worked-up, horny, neediness, I'm pleased that she trusts me.

"Imagine what it would feel like for me to slide into you—for my cock to sink, inch by inch, until I bottom out. *Fuck*," I can hardly get the words out. "Imagine your tight, warm cunt taking me, tightening around me. Shit, you have no idea what I would do to feel you coming all over my cock."

Her teeth bite into her bottom lip, and that is the beginning of the end.

Everything swells, and my muscles ripple under my skin.

A string of mumbled nonsense streams from my mouth as everything bursts.

"Open your eyes," I beg with my last bit of coherent thought. When she opens her eyes, that's all I can take. I come all over her stomach as she watches.

Both of us are breathing loudly, our chests rising and falling rapidly as we suck in air.

Falling onto the bed beside her, I feel exhaustion taking hold.

As my eyes drift close, her stomach rumbles. What was meant to be time for a nap has come and gone. It must be getting close to dinner time.

"Let's go get you something to eat."

"Let's nap first," she yawns.

A warm feeling travels from my stomach to my chest. She's so tired that she doesn't have the energy to feel embarrassed by what we just did. I'll let her sleep, maybe she'll let me hold her.

CHAPTER 19

 naïs

MY EYES FLUTTER open and everything that happened floods my mind like a tidal wave.

Oh my God!

The memory of his tongue makes me feel warm.

Pulling the sheet down, I realize I'm naked.

Oh my God!

Quickly pulling the sheet up again, I freeze in the pitch-black room. A large hand comes down on my stomach, and Kane mumbles something before taking a deep sighing breath.

He's asleep.

Wide awake in the dark, I try to process what happened earlier. He wanted to have sex with me. Much to my own shock, I actually wanted to have sex with him too. Whatever

95

he did with his mouth melted my brain. I was momentarily dumbstruck.

That explains it.

I blush thinking about his face between my legs. The way he moaned like it was the most delicious thing he ever tasted makes me curious. I wonder what he tastes like.

Sheesh. One orgasm, and it's like a switch was flipped in my brain.

Even now I can feel that fluttering, wet, tingly sensation in my stomach. I did research about orgasms, reading about them, but wow, no amount of reading prepared me for the real thing!

I couldn't control my body. Muscles tensing and shaking on their own. My mouth made sounds I never expected and couldn't stop. The way he stared, the hunger in his eyes, the noises he made while he licked me.

When he sat up and the towel fell away, I couldn't take my eyes off of him. Seeing him, hanging heavily between my legs was equally thrilling and terrifying. I can't imagine that he would fit inside of me. Thinking about it makes me jittery and excited.

Seeing it so close, I could have reached out and touched it. My eyes flutter closed as I remember it. So smooth looking. A thick vein runs from the bottom almost all the way to the top. Before he came, the tip looked swollen and shiny.

His hand moves on my stomach, pressing down a bit harder, and I have to stifle a groan.

Just feeling his skin against mine makes me want more.

I need to get out of this bed. His soft breaths are making me want to reach out and hold him.

I wonder if he would be alright with that.

Sliding out of his silk sheets without waking him is a strange process. I let my legs slip to the ground while my back is still flat on the mattress. Then, slowly, I turn, letting his large hand rest on the bed. Slinking away, I search the darkness for my robe.

I find a t-shirt. It smells like him, clean and strong. Pulling it over my head, I leave the room as quietly as I can.

The large windows reveal deep night skies full of stars. How long had we slept?

I'll cook! I don't know about a lot of the ingredients he has, but I'm sure I can figure something out.

It takes me a while to find the light switches in the kitchen, which doesn't bode well, but I'm determined. Using almost nothing, I was always able to create something out of the bits and scraps my dad brought home.

I've only ever cooked canned meat, so real, fresh, raw bacon is frightening, but I've seen him eat it before, and I know he likes it.

Thoughts of last night linger in the back of my mind. I don't want to think about it anymore, it makes me too anxious. When he wakes, I have no idea what to do. Is he going to want to talk about it? Or try to do it again? Is he going to act like it never happened? Will he be done with me now that he's drawn sexual pleasure from my body?

He still hasn't answered when I've asked him why he has me with him.

The thought is distressing. Returning back to The Playground and continuing to work down my debts would be almost unbearable now. He's still an enigma, a tightly wrapped mystery, but the more time we spend together, the more I want to know everything about him. I wonder how many people know him well enough to know that he spins the ring on his left thumb when he's thinking. Or that he has a truly beautiful smile when his guard drops enough to let one show. Or that he takes three sugars and no cream in his coffee. Or that when he thinks no one is around, he hums, softly. Or the face he makes when he comes.

Trying to focus on the task at hand, I push the thoughts down, letting them boil and fester at the base of my skull.

Using a fork to flip a piece of bacon, I yelp and jump back when the grease pops and singes my hand.

"Ouch!"

I pout angrily at the pan.

A deep chuckle from behind me startles me again.

"What are you doing?"

Holding my chest, I turn to face him. He's smiling—one of those rare, big, beautiful ones.

"Making you breakfast." I gesture to the cut fruits and bowl of whisked eggs on the counter.

"It's two in the morning." He's still smiling.

"Oh." I look around at the food, suddenly feeling embarrassed. "We didn't eat dinner, so I thought—" My voice trails.

"You didn't have dinner," he smirks. "I ate a delicious meal."

My cheeks burn bright red, and my thighs squeeze together.

"I'm definitely hungry," his smirky, arrogant smile changing to a genuine one. "I can take over the bacon if you want."

When he steps behind me, taking the fork from my hand, the heat from his body radiates against my back.

"You look so good in my shirt," he growls against the shell of my ear.

I'm hot and flustered by his closeness. I take a disoriented step back, right into the hardness of his body. In a flash, his arm is around my waist, holding me tightly against him with his hand tightly cupping my sex. If the shirt wasn't so long, he would be touching bare, naked skin.

I gasp and lean into him further. What is wrong with me?

He's hard against my back, I can feel his hips pressing forward, pushing himself into me.

When I whine, he moans and brings his mouth down to my neck. His soft lips and hot tongue suck the sensitive skin. Wet heat pools between my legs, right where his hand is holding me.

"K-Kane, I think we should, maybe, wait. I'm-" scared, afraid, terrified, confused, all of the above.

"What is distressing you?" his whisper crawls across my neck.

"Why am I here? Why did you take me out of The Playground? Why am I staying here with you? Why did you bring me, of all people, up top with you?" The words spill out like vomit—sour and uncontrollable, driven by the swirling confusion and fear that have been festering.

Once I start everything spills out and I can't stop it.

He moves his hand up to rest on my stomach and takes a short step back.

"I want you to be mine," he says too calmly.

"Your what?" I don't understand.

"Mine. My woman, the queen beside me, my wife. Whatever you want to be, you will be." His tone is unwavering.

The words hit me like a physical blow, and nausea churns in my gut. I can barely breathe. It's like he's laid out a future I never asked for, a life that feels like another prison.

"What?" I yank myself free from his grip, putting as much distance as possible between us in the small space.

"Why are you angry?" His brows knit together, genuine confusion marring his features. He truly doesn't understand.

"So, you take me from The Playground and keep me in

your house. Do I have any choice here? Any say whatsoever?" My voice rises with every word, the anger bubbling over. My entire body shakes with the force of it.

"Do you not want to be mine?" There's a softness in his voice now, a vulnerability that makes me question everything.

"I don't know!" I scream, throwing my hands up in the air. "How can I possibly know? You're talking about making me your wife? We barely know each other! I've been out of the prison that was my father's house for a few weeks, and now you want to lock me away in your penthouse!"

"You know me better than almost anyone," he counters.

"I know your favorite book and color," I feel crazy. That's almost nothing! That can't possibly be enough information to know that you want someone to be yours, right?

There must be more to it than that.

"Exactly," he says, almost desperately, as if that simple knowledge is enough. "No one else knows those things."

My stomach churns. Even though I don't know him, I do. I think back to his quiet humming, and guilt grips my insides.

"I just need time to process this." Turning on my heels, I quickly run up to my room.

What is the polar opposite of fickle? How can he be so sure of what he wants? There was no doubt in his voice —he was so steady, so sure.

How?

Stripping his shirt from my body I go immediately to the shower. I need to wash all traces of him from my skin. I catch a glimpse of my neck in the mirror.

Fantastic.

He sucked an angry red bruise just under my jaw.

CHAPTER 20

 Kane

FUCK.

That did not play out how I envisioned it in my head.

I'm the ruler of The Underworld. I don't ask people what they want or check in with how my decisions make them feel. I do what I please, and they fall in line.

I suppose that was where I made a mistake here.

I don't want to rule over her. I want her to stand beside me, to rule beside me.

Turning off the stove, I pace the length of the kitchen. My confusion is simmering under my skin. I am the King of Hell. I say jump, and people say "how high" or I blow their fucking brains out. The simmering increases, full boiling rage taking its place.

Swiping my arm across the counter, the bowl of whisked

eggs flies across the room. A viscous trail of yellow slime coats the counter, floor, and wall.

"Fuck!"

I need to leave. She asked for space, and if I stay in this house one second longer, I won't give it to her. I want to storm up there and break her door off its hinges and demand to know why she doesn't want me.

I knew I wanted her instantly. Obviously, she doesn't feel the same way.

The door slams behind me, shaking the windows. As soon as my feet hit the sand, I break into a sprint. Running through the soft, resistant sand will help clear my mind. The beach is desolate, with only the sound of water crashing against the shore.

She said she 'needs time to process.' I don't really know what that means, but I can give her space. I don't process things, I react immediately. She's not like me, though. She's soft and thoughtful. That's why I like her so much. I could see her tenderness the first time I laid eyes on her, and it drew me in.

I just wasn't expecting her to get angry. I thought, after last night, that she would be glad to hear that I don't just want some fuck toy, but a partner.

Fuck.

I stop running, so far down the beach, I can't even see the house.

I am going to give her space, to let her think about everything, and not bully her into a hasty decision. I need to show her that she does have a say in everything. Her opinion matters more to me than anyone else's.

Pulling my phone from my pocket, I call Declan.

"Sir?" he's groggy.

"I need you to set up another throne in the judgment

room."

"Another throne?"

"Yes, make it exactly like mine, place it beside mine."

"Yes, Sir."

"I want this completed by the time I return."

"By tomorrow night?" His tone is skeptical.

An angry growl rumbles in my throat.

"Who the fuck are you questioning? Tell them I want it in place when I get home tomorrow, I don't care if it takes twenty people working down to the minute that I return. If it's not in the judgment room when I get there, everyone involved will spend two weeks in the pits, and then I'll blow a fucking hole through your skulls. Am I being clear?"

"Y-Yes, sir," I can hear rustling and movement on his end.

"Good."

What the fuck has gotten into him? He's lasted as my valet longer than anyone else because of his normally stoic, emotionless nature. His questioning tones and confused facial expressions are starting to piss me off.

Or maybe I'm just upset that Anaïs didn't leap into my arms and onto my cock when I made my intentions clear.

I walk, slow and sulking back toward the house. As I walk, the sun starts to peek over the horizon.

A man with a fluffy-looking white rat dog walks past me. The dog runs around my ankles and jumps up, putting its wet, sandy paws on my knees.

"Get it off." I grit toward the man whose cheery smile falls as he looks at my face.

"Oh, I'm sorry, she's really friendly." He hurries to grab the animal away.

After a few steps, a thought comes to mind.

"Hey!" I turn back to the man who looks startled.

"Women like dogs, right?"

His brow furrows, and he clutches the animal in his arms like I'm going to fucking snatch it.

"Um... I guess it depends on the woman." He looks completely unsure.

Fucking useless.

Taking out my phone I start to search, clearly, I will have to handle this myself since everyone else is incompetent.

When I finally make it back to the house, the sun is shining, which only adds to my gloom. I have to fight the urge not to knock on her door.

She needs time and space.

After showering, I make a few calls while lying in bed. My hand instinctively moves over the area where she slept. Where the wetness from between her legs dripped down into the sheets.

How much distance is needed for "space," and how much time does one need to "process?" Are a few hours sufficient?

I should let her come to me.

Careful to include everything, I send detailed instructions to Zion. He will get the job done but if I'm not clear he'll fuck it up somehow.

Tossing my phone down, I stare up at the ceiling.

This is worse than being incurably bored. This awful itch, my body jitters, and I'm restless and on edge. She's just one floor above me. Right over my head.

Ringing momentarily distracting me from my misery. Until I see the name on the screen.

Fucking Zion.

My misery returns in full force.

"What."

"Hello, dearest brother. I am throwing a party on Saturday night. I know you won't want to but you have to attend."

"Why?"

"Because it's for your fucking birthday, Kane. I'll drag you from your home if necessary."

I'm already in a bad mood, he's making it worse.

"Plus, I'm doing you a huge favor. This is how you can repay me." He sounds smug.

"I wouldn't call it a *huge* favor." It's one simple task.

"I would. Bring Babydoll, she'll love it!"

"Stop calling her that. Get the fuck job done and I'll think about it." I hang up and silence the phone. If she is speaking to me, I'll ask her if she would like to go.

CHAPTER 21

 naïs

UNLIKE LAST TIME I packed this suitcase, I am not rushing. I take each item and fold it carefully, placing everything so that it is packed thoughtfully. Stalling.

I don't want to leave. I don't want to sit beside him in the backseat for hours.

We haven't talked since yesterday morning. I told him that I needed time to process, then he disappeared. I came down a few hours later when I was too hungry to ignore it. There was food prepared, but he wasn't around. At the time, I was grateful. By lunch, the feeling had diminished. When dinner rolled around and he was still nowhere to be found, I went to his room.

I stood outside the closed door, my balled-up fist in midair, ready to knock. I just couldn't do it.

What was I planning to say?

I feel like I'm drowning in so many emotions I can't fight my way to the surface.

I didn't want him to use me and then discard me, but this doesn't feel like the better alternative. What he's suggesting he wants marriage? The fact that he is the Ruler of The Underworld, aside, marriage to anyone is a huge commitment.

I do feel something for him. When I see him, something stirs in my chest—something warm and secure. There is always a trembling nervousness around him, a fluttery excitement just being near him. I have a crush on him.

I've also been gripped by the fear that he wants to use me and throw me away or that he's playing some sick game with me.

What would it mean to be his? Am I a prisoner in his house? If I decide I don't want him, do I just go back to The Playground?

Will he accept that I want more time to get to know him, or are the options marriage or nothing?

My stomach rumbles, but I can't eat. The tense knots will only allow a few small bites of food before I'm nauseous. My entire body aches, the stiffness in my muscles from lack of sleep, and the constant anxious feeling is getting to me.

I know we need to talk, but I don't know what to say.

I feel like an idiot. Despite my misgivings over his offer, I'm disappointed each time I look for him and he's not there. In an unexplainable way, I miss him.

Despite the fear, he somehow makes me feel safe. I truly believe that he would never let physical harm come to me. I've heard him, yelling, angry, and commanding, but never with me. With me, he's gentle.

He touches me with care, like I might break if his grip is too rough.

Even the way he looks at me is soft. There have been moments of lust and desire, times I thought he was going to devour me, and he has.

There are moments when I catch him staring, it makes my stomach flip just thinking about it. He looks at me in a way no one else ever has, with admiration.

The interactions that I've had with men have been few, but they left a lot to be desired.

My father was a drunk with a gambling problem. As long as the house was clean, his meals were prepared, and I was quiet, we usually didn't have any problems. The men at The Playground looked at me in a way that made my skin prickle and crawl. It made me feel dirty and ashamed.

Kane makes me feel small but not lesser. He is formidable, in both mentality and stature. He is wise to the ways of the world, The Underworld in particular. He runs it. He controls every wild, vile thing without fear or hesitation.

Yet with me, he is affectionate. He touches me, his large hands grazing my leg, my shoulder, and my hand. A shiver runs over my skin at the thought. Even a nonsexual touch is exciting.

Pulling the suitcase shut, I sprint across the hall and down the stairs. Whatever happens, we need to talk. I can't process this until I fully understand all of it.

Rolling my shoulders back and taking a breath, I knock on his door loud enough to appear confident. With the footsteps behind the door, my hands tremble a little bit, so I ball them into fists by my sides.

My face falls instantly when the door is opened.

"Miss Poulain," his manservant, is as serious and aloof as ever.

"Can I talk to Kane?" I've finally worked up the nerve, but I wasn't expecting this. I didn't plan for it.

"I'm afraid he's already departed, Miss. I am packing his belongings and then driving you down."

"Oh." I'm crushed. Admittedly, I had been dreading the tense, possibly silent car ride, but he's skipping it altogether? I feel particularly small and stupid standing here in front of him.

"Will you be able to leave in the next fifteen minutes?"

"Yes, I'll be downstairs."

After turning and taking a few steps, I decide to ask, "Did he say why?" I start, looking back to find the door already closed.

With sulky steps, I walk down to the first floor. Sliding the glass door open, I stand on the deck, leaning on the railing. The salty breeze and warm sun soothe the ache just a bit.

Closing my eyes, I tilt my face up to feel the sun on my face. The hot, orange glow against my eyelids feels strange and wonderful.

We haven't left, and I already miss it.

"Miss Poulain?"

"I'm ready," my shoulders slump as I walk inside, taking one second to stare at the water for the last time.

We've barely driven from the driveway when the partition that separates the front from the backseats comes down.

"I'm Declan," he eyes me in the rearview mirror.

"I'm Anaïs."

"It's nice to meet you. If you need anything or would like to stop anywhere, I have been instructed to do whatever you want."

I nod, rolling my lips into my mouth to force them to behave. I want to ask him a million questions. He must know

109

so much about Kane. I can't ask him to breach his boss' trust like that.

We drive in silence through the wide-open valley, across the treelined highway, past the mountains, and toward the bridge. My heart hurts as we approach it. I almost ask him to slow down, just to prolong the inevitable for a few moments more.

Despite my sadness to leave, the bridge still stirs the same sense of awestruck wonder. It blooms in my chest and forces a smile to my lips.

The rest of the drive passes by in an upsettingly fast blur.

As we enter the tunnel into The Underworld I find myself holding my breath.

We bypass the line of buses and security vehicles. What's the rush?

The trilling sound of a phone ringing loudly over the car speakers makes me jump.

"Declan," It's Kane, and he sounds off.

"Sir, we just-"

"Don't bring her down here!" He cuts him off as the rapid sound of gunfire erupts through the speaker.

"Sir, we're here! We're through the security roundabout." His voice is tight.

"Fuck! Take her to Hanzo's and hide her. If anything happens to her, Declan... "

"Yes, Sir. I understand."

The car swerves hard left, turning across the lanes of oncoming traffic. Tires screeching, horns blaring, the sound of the motor accelerating, everything is blurry.

Declan drives the car at an unnervingly fast rate of speed on the wrong side of the road, weaving in and out of the lanes.

"Everything is going to be alright, Miss Poulain. You'll be safe at Hanzos."

Somehow I doubt that very much. While I've never been there, my father frequented that establishment often. He would, more often than not, lose all of our money there, then take out a loan that he couldn't repay. Hanzo's men love to collect unpaid debts with nightsticks and baseball bats.

The car lurches forward as he slams on the brakes in front of a multi-level wooden structure.

"Come," he rips my door open and holds his hand out to me. I have to run in a near-full sprint to keep up with him as he holds me tightly under his arm.

A large man in a suit eyes us but says nothing as he holds the door open.

"Where is Hanzo?" Declan asks once we're inside.

"Declan," a voice comes from the shadowy corner of the room. "I must say I'm surprised to see you here. Who is this?"

The man that steps into the dim light makes my blood run cold. He is tall and lanky, his long, stringy hair falls limply down to his shoulders. Puffs of cigar smoke linger around him like a grimy cloud.

"Kane needs her safe. We will wait in Hanzo's office until his arrival."

We follow the creepy man up the stairs to a metal door. The door is riddled with strange circular indentions.

"Bullets," Declan whispers when he notices me staring.

I gulp and step closer to him.

One wall in the room is covered in computer monitors, at least forty of them. In the gambling rooms, men sat wasting their money, covering each screen.

"Where is Hanzo?" Declan asks the sinister man.

"At the poker tables," he smiles at me, his thick yellowed teeth on full display.

My mind races with a million horrific ways that Kane could be in trouble. Doesn't he need Declan with him, to protect him?

"Hey," Declan whispers, "he will be here soon. Don't worry."

Easier said than done.

CHAPTER 22

 Kane

Bullets ricochet off the car that I'm using as a cover. There are only two of them left, but they are definitely doing damage.

Loading my gun I lean against the car door and close my eyes. Focusing to pinpoint the origin of the shots that are raining down on us.

I need to hurry up and end this, Anaïs is here, at Hanzos, and she's probably afraid. I need to make sure she's safe.

Taking a deep breath, I slide back the bolt and make sure that there's a round in the chamber.

I can see one of my security guards crouching behind the door inside the security kiosk. We make eye contact, he nods, as ready as I am.

Holding up three fingers, I count them down slowly, and

we both jump up, firing until the magazines are empty. The remaining men lay in expanding pools of blood.

After checking to make sure there's no one else, I quickly search a few of the bodies. I need something, anything. Identification, a phone, something that will give me an indication of who ordered this attack.

Four of my guards are dead and another is wounded.

"Take me to Hanzo's now," I'm barely keeping my rage in check.

"Right away, sir," he nods, stepping over the bodies that litter the ground.

"I want a full investigation," I turn to the remaining men. "I want to know who ordered this hit, why, and how the fuck they got into my secure garage! Call Zion, he's leading this!"

"Yes, sir!"

If I didn't need to get to her, I would probably kill all of them. How the fuck did this happen? My home, all the way down to my personal garage, is supposed to be an impenetrable fortress.

This kid is new, I can tell by how nervous he is. I can see his hands shaking as he weaves through the streets. The car is jerky, stopping and accelerating in rough transitions.

I would be annoyed if I didn't have so much on my mind.

Before the car comes to a complete stop, I'm jumping out and rushing toward the door. Sharp pain in my side knocks the air out of my lungs, forcing me to lean against the door for a moment.

"Sir," he tries.

"Not now..."

I push through the pain and take the back stairs two at a time.

"Dec," I shout, and the metal door immediately clanks open.

I see her over his shoulder, frightened and small.

She gasps when she sees me, then jumps to her feet.

"Kane!" She studies me carefully, the rims of her eyes filling with tears.

"It's not mine," I whisper in reassurance, but I know she doesn't believe me.

It might have been a wise idea to wipe some of the blood off in the car on the way over.

"We're leaving now." I hold her hand in mine and lead her out of the room. Even seeing her in a place like this makes my skin crawl. The Playground was bad enough.

"Kane?" Her voice is soft, like it was before, like she's afraid to speak to me. "Are you alright? What happened?"

When we reach the car and she's safely out of Hanzos, I slide into the middle seat beside her.

"I was ambushed in my personal parking garage," I try to control my voice. "Zion is trying to find out what happened." I hope that will ease the worried crease between her eyes.

"You're hurt," her small hand comes up to gently touch my blood-soaked shirt.

"I'll be fine."

She sniffles and drops her head down.

"Whoa, everything is going to be alright. I will always keep you safe," I slide my finger under her chin and tip her head up to look at her.

"I was mad at you," her voice cracks, "I was upset about what you said in the kitchen; I was angry that you've been distant since. I was mad that you left without me today. What if they had killed you and our last conversation was a fight? What if you died and I was angry at you?"

"I was giving you space. I was being distant because I thought you wanted that."

Females are fucking confusing.

"I know, I needed to think and process, but I looked for you. I didn't want you to disappear." She stops and looks down at her hands. "I guess I did ask for space."

Declan keeps trying to sneak a glance at us in the mirror. I clench my jaw and narrow my eyes at him, and he quickly looks forward.

"Are you sure you're alright? There is so much blood." Her wide eyes meet mine, and everything that was painful and sharp goes numb.

"I'm fine. I may need a stitch or two."

Her soft fingers move across my cheek, wiping the blood away.

The car comes to a stop behind my building. Declan was smart enough to know not to bring her down into the garage.

I slide out of my seat, biting into my lip to keep from making any sounds of discomfort.

"Yo! What the fucking fuck, man?" Zion's voice is angry, booming, as soon as I close the door.

"Zion," I move my eyes back and forth between his and Anaïs, hoping he will understand and shut the fuck up.

"You shouldn't have killed them all, we could have tortured one for information!" He wipes his bloody hands on a towel. "It's a fucking mess down there, fucking brains everywhere."

Anaïs whimpers beside me.

Jesus Christ, this idiot!

I pull her into my side, holding her trembling body safely against mine.

"It had to be Farly," Zion snarls angrily as he looks over my blood-stained clothes. "No one else would have had the balls, man."

"That's what I'm thinking too."

I feel her arm around my waist, holding me. I force back the flinch my body does involuntarily at the pressure from her hand. I don't want her to drop her arm, even if it hurts.

"Let's get upstairs, we shouldn't be standing out in the open like this," Zion holds the door open.

I feel her tense at his words, her head swiveling back and forth to look for oncoming threats.

As we ride the crowded elevator up to the penthouse, my heart starts to pound in my chest. I wasn't nervous at first, but now that we're almost there, I'm second-guessing my decisions.

It's too late now. I take a deep breath as the doors slide open.

CHAPTER 23

 naïs

As the elevator doors open, I notice Oksana immediately. She's sitting on the couch with a frightened look on her face until she sees me.

She jumps up from her seat as I run towards her, colliding into each other's open arms.

"What are you doing here?" I squeeze her tightly.

"I don't know!" she chuckles. "Zion brought me here this morning. Said to sit down on this couch, and I've been sitting here ever since!"

"Sorry about that," Zion chimes in from behind us, "things got a bit busy, and I forgot you were up here."

I look at Kane, who is staring at me with a solemn look on his face, like he's studying me.

"Are you pleased?" His usual confidence looks shaken. He looks unsure of himself.

Before I can respond, a trembling woman steps out from the hallway at the top of the stairs. She's holding something small and black in her arms. It wiggles and moves as she nervously walks down the steps toward us.

It's a puppy. What is going on?

Kane takes it from the woman who looks like she might pass out.

"I got you this," he says, placing the tiny black dog in my arms. "His name is Jinx."

The puppy wiggles and licks my cheek. He's so cute it makes my eyes water.

"You got this for me?"

"Yes, when he's fully grown, he will be a reliable guard dog. He'll protect you when I'm not around."

I look at the puppy in my arms. His ears and the end of his short tail have bandages wrapped around them.

"His tail was docked and his ears were cropped yesterday. I have an ointment that you'll need to put on them to keep them clean and free of infection." He must have noticed my concern.

I nod, not sure what to say.

He got me a dog!

"Do you like him? Do you want to keep him?" He seems unsure again.

Do I like him? Is he joking?

I'm not sure what to say, so I lunge forward and wrap my free arm around his waist. His arms wrap around me quickly, holding me in the embrace until Zion clears his throat.

As I look up at him, I see Oksana standing beside him. Both of them are looking at me with the same expression. The picture of shock and disbelief.

"I have some business to attend to," his voice is gravelly

and tired. "Oksana will be staying in the room across the hall from yours."

I jerk back to look at him.

"She's staying here?" "I'm staying here?" We both speak at the same time.

"You said she was your friend," he states, like I should somehow be aware of these new developments after saying that. "You said you missed her. Would you not like her to stay here?"

"If she would like to stay here, of course, I would like that." I look toward her shocked face.

"Stay here, as in live here?" Her mouth is hanging open.

"Yes, my, um, Anaïs wants you here." He looks down at me and corrects himself, "if you would like to stay you can." His words come out slowly, as if he's never cared about someone else's feelings before.

Oksana quirks her brow and looks at me. She keeps blinking like she's trying to tell me something in code.

My shoulders shrug slightly. I don't know what she wants me to do.

"Thank you, Sir," she finally answers, "I would like to stay."

I bounce on my toes, too excited to control myself. Jinx lets out a small whiny sound, and I press a small kiss to the side of his nose.

"Come, I'll show you his bed and ointment," Kane places his hand on the small of my back, guiding me upstairs.

"Don't forget the shit garden!" Zion chuckles.

"The shit garden?"

"Don't you have work to do?" Kane snaps at his brother before turning to me. "I ordered a small plot of synthetic grass to be placed on the balconies so that we don't have to take him all the way down the stairs every time…" His voice trails off.

"You thought of everything," My cheeks hurt from smiling.

"Shit garden," Oksana whispers to herself as her shoulders shake with laughter.

"I'll give you a few minutes," she whispers as we reach the top of the stairs. I watch for a moment as she follows Zion down the hallway to her door.

My room looks the same with the addition of a dog bed in the corner. I can feel Kane behind me, standing just inside the doorway.

After setting Jinx down, I turn to him, our chests almost touching. He looks upset.

"What's wrong? Are you sure you aren't hurt?"

He brings his hands to my waist before pressing a small kiss on my forehead.

"I had hoped, when we came back from the beach, that you would want to move into my room."

"Oh…"

"I have a few things to take care of," he stops me before I try to explain that I'm not ready for that yet. "I'll be back tonight. I'm leaving Declan here, so if you need anything, just ask."

He turns to leave, but I grab his hand.

"Kane, please be careful. Whatever happened today with Farly, just please, promise me you will be safe."

"How do you know about Farly?"

Cohen Farly, Everyone knows about Cohen Farly. Even me. He is as notorious as Kane.

"I've lived down here my whole life, I've heard of him."

He hums and rubs his thumb over my finger. "Can I bring you somewhere tomorrow?"

"Yes."

The crease between his brows slowly fades away with my answer. I guess that means he's happy?

"I'll see you later. Remember, if you need anything—"

"Ask Declan." I smile up at him as Jinx runs between our feet.

"Kane..." I stop him again as he opens the door. I know he needs to leave, but I can't shake the feeling in the pit of my stomach. I don't want him to go.

Stepping forward, I wrap my arms around him again. He tenses for a moment then wraps his arms around me.

"Thank you for Jinx and for bringing Oksana here. You don't know what it means to me."

"You're happy?"

"Yes."

"Good," he says as he brings his hand to my hair, running his fingers through it before backing out of the room.

CHAPTER 24

 naïs

I'm SITTING on the floor playing with Jinx when there is a light tap on the door.

"Anaïs?" Oksana whispers.

"Come in!"

She tiptoes into the room and closes the door with comical care. Turning the knob slowly so that there is no sound.

"What is going on?" she whispers again.

"Why are you whispering?"

"I'm in Kane Azraels house. What the fuck is going on?" She looks bewildered.

"Sit down!" I pat the floor beside me.

"When Honey told me that he took you after your dance, when you never came back, I thought you were dead," she sits beside me.

123

"He just," I don't know what to say. On one hand, I could really use some advice. On the other hand, he might not be too thrilled about other people knowing about what he said. "He just brought me here to stay with him."

"Pussy power." she nods her head. Am I supposed to know what that means?

"Pussy power?"

"Yeah, you know. When a man is so infatuated with the pussy that you hold all the power. We see it all the time at The Playground. Men will do just about anything for good pussy." She's very matter-of-fact about this.

"We haven't had sex." Now I'm the one that's whispering.

"What?" She looks shocked. "Well, what have you been doing all this time?"

"I don't know, just hanging out."

"Why did he bring me here?" She looks confused.

"I told him about you, that you're my friend, and that I missed you."

"Wait, let me get this straight." She rises slowly from the ground and starts walking around the room. "You told him that you missed me, and now he's moving me into his penthouse mansion in the sky...because you missed me."

"Yes, because I missed you," I laugh.

"Girl, he is in love with you. This goes way beyond pussy. He's moving your friend into his house and buying you dogs! Holy shit!"

"I should probably put some ointment on Jinx," I try to change the subject.

"No way, sister, you're not getting out of this that easily. Has he said anything to you? How do you feel about him?"

I haven't even talked to him about how I feel about him.

"Ok, ok, I get it," she laughs and kisses Jinx. "Keep your

secrets. I will say this though, and then I'll shut up, you look different."

"Different?"

"Yeah, just... different."

I'm grateful for her company as the hours fade into night. If she wasn't here, I would be sitting by the door, waiting for him to come back. I'm worried that he's in danger again. Maybe they were ambushed again. Or someone could have betrayed him. Betrayal in The Underworld is as commonplace as breathing.

I find myself pacing my room, unable to keep still.

I don't even know where his room is. I never accepted any of the offers for a tour of the house.

Slipping out into the dark hallway, I creep down to the end, opening all of the doors I pass except Oksana's. Another bedroom, a gym, and an office.

Holding a sleeping Jinx tight to my chest, I start down the staircase. The whirling of gears makes me freeze halfway down. There is nowhere to hide, I'm right out in the open.

The elevator door opens, and Kane steps out.

He's looking down, he hasn't seen me yet.

"Kane! You're hurt!" The words fly out of my mouth.

His head jerks up at the sound of my voice.

"I'm fine. Why are you awake? Are you alright?"

"I was looking for you," I jog the remaining steps. "You are hurt! Don't lie to me!"

I can see it in his posture, in his walk. He doesn't hang his head, his shoulders don't slump, and he doesn't take small steps.

He's not wearing the same blood-stained shirt as earlier. Through the thin material of his t-shirt, I can see a bandage around his chest. With care, I reach up and let the tips of my fingers touch it.

"What happened here?"

He closes his eyes and leans into my touch, "it's just a graze, no big deal, barely broke the skin."

"A graze? Like… a bullet?"

I feel panicky. A bullet was this close to his chest, to his heart.

"Hey," he runs his hand over my cheek and back through my hair, holding the back of my head. "I'm fine, Anaïs. Please, don't be concerned."

"You need to rest. Where is your room?"

He sighs and leads me toward a small hallway behind the stairs. His room is as big as the entire second floor. My throat feels dry as we step inside. His room is massive. The bed in the center almost looks like a throne, a carved black wooden four-poster with black silk sheets. He sleeps here. Right in this spot. He lays his big, powerful body down, right here.

"Lie down," my voice is embarrassingly squeaky.

I may not be ready to marry him, but that doesn't stop my mind from wandering to all of the things we could do in a bed this size.

He's injured. I'm sure that is the last thing on his mind.

He lifts his arm to pull his shirt off, and a pained grimace flashes over his face before he composes himself.

"Can I put him down on your bed?" I nod down to Jinx. "Yes."

After freeing my hands, I stand in front of him, taking the hem of his shirt between my fingers. This isn't sexual. He's hurt, and I'm helping him.

I'm undressing him.

My breath is shaky as I carefully pull the shirt up, moving it over his good side before slowly moving the material over his neck and down the arm on his bad side.

"Thank you," his voice is low.

"Do you, um, what about your pants?"

"Do you want to take my pants off, Anaïs?" His voice is still low, but there is a hint of teasing amusement.

"If you need help," I try to sound confident, but my heart is pounding in my throat.

"Please."

With shaking fingers, I reach for his belt. After some tugging and pulling, it opens. The button pops open easily. I feel sweat accumulating on the back of my neck. It's so hot in his room.

As my fingers pull the zipper down, I feel them graze over the hard bulge just under my hand.

A low groan vibrates in his chest.

The pants pool around his ankles, and he kicks them to the side.

"G-Get in bed." I have to clear my throat.

I hurry in front of him, propping pillows up against the headboard for him to lean back on. He sits slowly, leaning back against the pillows.

I know he's hurt and he needs to rest, but I don't want to leave. Earlier he mentioned wanting me to move into his room. Maybe he won't mind if I stay, just for tonight.

"Um, Kane," I'm so nervous, "can I stay here with you tonight?"

"You can stay with me whenever you want to. I told you I wanted you to move in here. You don't have to ask."

With a nervous chuckle and red cheeks, I awkwardly climb over his legs and into the bed beside him.

"What happened today?"

He sighs and slides his hand over the sheets until he finds mine.

"Cohen Farly is trying to kill me to take my place as ruler."

Fear wraps around my chest, squeezing my lungs and making it hard to inhale.

"Don't worry, I'll be alright. He is hard to get to because of his fucking father. When I heard he was coming down here three years ago, I planned to get rid of him quickly. I knew he was going to cause trouble. His father provided him with such a huge entourage of security that my hands have been tied. I've kept him on my radar though. Why he's choosing to try this now, I'm not sure, but I'll figure it out."

"But what if you never get to him? What if he tries again?"

He chuckles, "He's a rich frat boy born with a silver spoon in his mouth. He's not half as smart as he thinks he is. He has no idea who he's fucking with."

He sounds so confident, but I'm still on edge. My dad used to talk about him, about how he got away with numerous atrocities up top because his father would pay off judges to keep him out of trouble. When it was finally too much to sweep under the rug, he was convicted and sent here. He had a huge loft built next to the pits because he wanted to be able to see it. Who wants to see the pits? Dad told me that he can hear people wailing and crying and that he *likes* it.

The thought makes my stomach turn.

"Hey," he squeezes my hand, "you're safe here. I will never let anything happen to you."

"What about you? Will you make sure nothing happens to you?" My heart squeezes at the thought.

"Nothing is going to tear me away from you. I'll be fine."

His answer makes my chest feel warm and fluttery. Careful not to touch his side, I lay my head on his shoulder and close my eyes. His soft breathing and thumping heart-beat lulling me to sleep.

CHAPTER 25

 ane

WELL, fuck.

She's sleeping beside me, laying on her stomach with her leg bent slightly. The large shirt she's wearing has bunched up around her hips. Her panty-clad ass is right beside my hand. It would hardly take any movement at all to reach over and grab it.

When she undressed me last night, I had a spark of hope that she would want to do more, but I could see her overriding concern over my wound.

She keeps fucking sighing in her sleep.

She straightens her legs, stretching her body. To keep myself from groaning, I bite into my lip.

She rolls over onto her side to face me, and the room is suddenly very warm.

Her face is almost eye level with my wide awake cock.

Her eyes go wide, and she sits up.

"Good morning," she whispers. Her eyes meet mine, but she keeps looking down.

"Good morning," my insides squeeze.

She stares down at her hands, her tongue swiping across her lips. I can feel her nervousness, but I can't pinpoint it. Is she uncomfortable? Is she thinking about the other night?

"Kane?" Her voice is small.

"Yeah, baby…"

"Can I-" she's blushing, "I want to touch you."

Jesus fucking Christ.

"Yes," a growl rumbles in my throat, "fuck, do whatever you want."

"Umm, ok. I'm just going to touch." Her soft fingers pull at the hem of my underwear. Flexing my hips forward, I lift enough for her to pull them down.

Oh, fuck me. This is happening.

Her eyes widen as my cock springs free, hanging above my stomach.

"Ok," she whispers to herself as she reaches her hand forward.

Everything feels like it's in slow motion. My heart pounds in my ears as I watch her timid hand wrap around the base of my erection.

She gasps, and I moan. My chest tenses sending sharp shooting pain through my ribs.

"Should I stop? I don't want to hurt you." She releases me, and a panic grips me. I'll beg her if I have to.

"No, please. I'm fine. I promise," my words come out rushed and frantic. "You could smash my ribs with a hammer for all I care; just please don't stop touching me." If she stops I'll die.

A small smile pulls at her lips.

When her hand grips me again, I sigh, relieved.

"Like this?" She moves her closed fist up and down over me.

"Fuck, yes, that's great, baby." I don't think she could do anything that doesn't feel amazing.

After a moment, she stops, still holding me but not moving her hand.

A rib-crushing, loud moan heaves from my bruised chest as she leans forward. Her tongue softly runs over my tip. She tentatively flicks over me, and I'm starting to feel lightheaded.

My fists grip the sheets so tightly that my knuckles turn white.

When she sucks the tip into her mouth, I can't even feel my ribs. My whole body is on fire, a bundle of raw, open nerves that are buzzing with electricity. Her mouth is so fucking wet and warm.

After swirling her tongue around for a moment, she moves her mouth down, taking more of me. Watching my cock sliding in and out of her mouth, saliva dripping down my shaft, is more than I can take.

I fist one of my hands into her hair, taking care not to push down on her head.

"Anaïs," my voice is raspy, begging.

She starts sucking gently, and I lose control, pumping my hips upward to meet her mouth. Every slurping suck from her hollowed-out mouth is better than the last. I'm freefalling into pleasure so deeply it's swallowing me whole.

Loud, rasping, heaving moans, and painful, sharp breathing sounds fill the room. A tightly coiled band snaps at the base of my spine, and my cock swells.

She looks up at me and slowly sinks her mouth down, taking just more than half of me.

"Fuck, Anaïs," I feel myself speaking, but I can't hear beyond my pulse. "Oh my fucking God."

I open my mouth to warn her, but it's too late. A gruff moan cuts off any attempt to speak as I shoot down the back of her throat.

Her eyes open wider, but she keeps her lips circled around me. When I stop twitching, she slides her mouth up and off.

For a moment she sits with her mouth closed. Her throat bobs as she swallows. Fuck.

My brain feels like scrambled eggs.

"Was that OK?" She's timid and shy.

"Anaïs..." I'm still breathless.

"I just wanted to return the favor, I guess. It didn't hurt you too much, did it? " Her fingers skim over the bandage.

"Come here," I grab her arm and pull her toward me.

"Kane! What are you doing? You're hurt! Stop it!" She's protesting, but I can hear the rasp in her voice, the breathiness that comes with being wound up tight.

"Sit on my face."

She gasps and pulls back, "What? No!"

"I'm not sure I can do it any other way, but I will if I have to." I pull her up, ignoring the objections from my body.

Her knees are on the mattress just above my shoulders, her legs bent so that the tops of her calves are under her on my shoulders and chest. I can feel her thighs tightening around my head as I pull her down. Hooking my finger into her soaking wet panties I pull them to the side.

"Fuck, you smell so good," I groan before licking a strip from bottom to top.

She moans and squirms above me.

I lick until she shakes until I can feel drops of her wetness rolling down the sides of my face. Her hips roll, grinding down against my mouth. The bashful woman who was worried about hurting me is no more.

Her hands come down into my hair, tugging tightly as I suck her clit.

"Kane!" she all but screams into the quiet room. Her back arching and her head falling back. I can feel the ends of her hair sweeping across my stomach.

"Oh my God," she whimpers as she crawls clumsily back down to her spot beside me.

"Do you still want to go out with me today?"

"Yes," she sounds tired again.

"It's judgment day, so I'll have to take care of that, but then after, I have somewhere to take you."

"Ok," she cuts herself off with a gasp. Sitting straight up in the bed. "Oh my God, Kane. Look at Jiji. He's just sitting there. Was he watching us the whole time?"

The puppy is sitting on the floor beside the bed, staring at us with his head cocked to one side.

"Wait, did you call him Jiji?"

"Yeah, it's cute."

"He's not meant to be cute. He's supposed to inspire fear in anyone who might consider targeting you."

"Do you think he was watching us?" She ignores me.

"It looks like it. It looks like he liked it."

She swats my arm. "He is a baby! He didn't know what we were doing."

"Or, he knew exactly what we were doing, and he liked it."

She groans and buries her face in the pillow.

I hope she sleeps with me again tonight.

CHAPTER 26

 naïs

MY HANDS knot together nervously as we ride the elevator up to the top floor of city hall, to the judgment room.

After this morning's activities, I would have liked to stay in bed, but I know he has a job to do. Hell doesn't stop just because I want him to stay home.

Declan is standing to my right, serious and threatening as ever.

"How many cases today?" Kane asks him.

"Thirty-two."

"Light day," he looks down at me and smiles. Thirty-two is a light day?

My stomach aches as we step out of the elevator into the cold, dark lobby.

Declan walks a few steps ahead as I drag my feet.

"What's the matter?" Kane stops walking and tilts my face toward him with his hand.

"Um, am I actually coming in with you? Or should I wait out here?" I hate this nervous feeling of not knowing where I'm supposed to be.

"You're coming with me." His brows furrow as if it would be ridiculous to even question that.

"Well, what do I do? Should I just stand in the back or next to Declan? I don't want to do the wrong thing."

"Anaïs, you sit with me."

I nearly choke. I'm going to sit with him? Where on his lap?

He starts walking toward the door that Declan is holding open for us. As we step into the room, I'm hit with an overwhelming sight.

The thirty-two people waiting to be judged are lined up along the back wall. Shackles around their wrists connect to a long chain that shackles their ankles. A majority of them are trembling, and some are already crying.

At the front of the room, two large thrones sit side by side, dead center.

I trip over my own feet. Luckily, his body mostly shields me from anyone seeing it.

He stops in front of the twin thrones and waits.

"Sit down," he whispers.

"Which one is for you?" I don't want to make a mistake in front of everyone.

He chuckles, deep and low. "Anaïs, they are exactly the same. Sit where you want."

I don't understand. Does he always have two thrones here? Or does he have a backup that they pulled out for the day? Where did this come from?

I sit down in one of the seats nervously. With his usual

confidence, he sits beside me, pulling my hand over into his on the armrest.

The crying has stopped, the occasional sniffle sounds through the room, but everything is eerily quiet. As I peek up, every single person, guards included, stares at our clasped hands wide-eyed and bewildered.

"First case," Kane waves his hand, and one of the guards unshackles a trembling woman and brings her to stand before us.

My heart lurches in my chest, her fear and crying squeezing my insides.

"Lorna Dune, charged with assault with a deadly weapon," Kane reads from a file in his lap. This small, scared-looking woman assaulted someone?

"Clearly, you did not learn from your two-month stint in the pits." Kane's voice is different. It's hard and cold. He almost sounds bored. "I don't give second chances. Miss Dune, you know this yet, here you are again, charged with the same offense."

"Please, Sir!" She drops to her knees and begs. "Please, I won't ever do it again. I was protecting myself! It was self-defense!"

I gasp and sit forward. Self-defense!

He hums and flips through the pages. "It says here you beat your girlfriend with a tire iron when she tried to break up with you."

"I, well," she breaks down, crying again.

"Death," Kane says with a voice so full of authority that it makes me tremble.

"No!" she wails, and I feel hot tears slide down my face. The metallic taste of blood fills my mouth as my teeth bite into my lip to keep myself quiet.

The King in Hell has made his ruling.

The click of his gun rings in my ears, and bile burns in my throat. Pinching my eyes closed, I brace myself. The echo of the shot reverberates through the marble hall, shaking me to my core.

I feel a hand on my arm, pulling me. Kane's voice sounds distant and muffled as I'm led away.

"Anaïs?"

"Anaïs?"

I force my eyes open. He's on his knees before me, his hands holding my face. We're outside the judgment room in the hallway.

"Anaïs?"

His face is distressed. The crease between his pulled-down brows is more prominent than usual.

"Why are you crying? What's the matter?"

"You killed her. She... is she dead?" I'm fully sobbing, each word choked out between hyperventilated breaths.

"Yes, baby, she was sentenced to death. I should have known your tender heart would be too sensitive for judgments," he growls.

"Please, don't be mad at me." I try to force myself to stop crying.

"I am angry with myself; I don't want to upset you."

"Why did she have to die? Couldn't she have gone to the pits instead?"

"She was sent to the pits last time she nearly beat someone to death. I have to have a zero tolerance for repeat offenders, Anaïs. People need to know that, even in The Underworld, there is law and order. Sex, drugs, gambling, and any number of vices are allowed here, out in the open, they are encouraged, in fact, but I cannot tolerate certain offenses. Murder, assault, rape... as a general rule, are immediate death sentences. If you commit those crimes up top and get sent down here, I allow them to live out their days unless they commit those offenses here. I won't stand for it."

"How do you do it? How do you shoot people and not feel torn up about it?"

"It's my job as ruler here to keep my subjects in line. I can't allow myself to be emotional because of a punishment that is handed down to a criminal." He shrugs his shoulders.

Stepping forward, I wrap my arms around his neck, letting the warmth from his body radiate into me.

"Let's go," I don't miss the way he winces when he stands. He puts on a strong front, no one else would know he has injuries. But I see it.

I turn to walk back into the judgment room, but he pulls me toward the elevator.

"We're not going back in there today."

"What about everyone that needs judgment?"

"It's done. Let's go." He steps into the elevator and holds his hand out to me.

I swallow nervously at what that means. It's done. I choose not to ask.

"Where are we going?" That's a safer question.

"Shooting."

CHAPTER 27

 ane

"WHAT ARE WE SHOOTING?" she finally asks as Declan pulls the car onto the street. I know she's been holding her tongue, but it's driving her crazy not knowing. In hindsight, this plan is probably a terrible idea after everything that just happened. I'm fucking up left and right here.

"Targets. I'm taking you to the gun range."

She exhales and visibly relaxes. My blood boils in my veins, hot and fucking furious. I made her cry. I scared her. I thought she would be happy. I thought I was showing her that she matters and that she will rule beside me.

The underground range is halfway between my office and our house. I only have a few minutes to prepare her. Swallowing my rage, I take her warm little hand in mine. It's still trembling slightly, and I wince.

"When we're in here, I need you to be careful, stay close

by me, and don't talk to anyone unless they come over to talk to us. It's early enough that it should be mostly empty, but just in case I want you to be careful."

She nods quickly, "I will."

"We'll be shooting two guns today. I just want you to be comfortable shooting them, even if you don't hit the target."

Her hand sits on her hip, and her brow quirks up. "What makes you think I won't be able to hit the target?" This little bit of cheeky attitude soothes my nerves. This is better than fear. She is playful, that is a good sign.

"I'm not doubting your abilities," a stupid smile spreads across my face. "I just know that this is your first time shooting, and it's not easy."

She leans in closer, looking to make sure the partition is closed. "I did something else for the first time today, and I would say that turned out pretty well."

My ribs ache as a painful laugh bursts from my chest. I didn't expect her to make a joke about that. She's usually so reserved. The more time I spend with her, the more I want to spend. She is all things good and sweet, but there is fire underneath.

"I'm sorry," she reaches out and touches my jacket, "don't hurt yourself." Her sweet nature returns quickly.

"Don't apologize, you're right, I shouldn't underestimate you. You are quite capable."

The blush that sweeps across her cheeks always stirs my heart. I'm not sure I like it. It feels soft and fluttering, not sensations I generally enjoy. I assume that this is what some kind of arrhythmia feels like.

Declan pulls the car into park. There is only one other vehicle in the lot. Good.

Anaïs has a bit of bounce in her step as we enter. The elevator takes us down below ground.

She marvels at the range, the sparkling curiosity and excitement have returned to her eyes. My fuck up this morning was unforgivable. I should have known she would be upset at the judgments.

My guilt is only slightly assuaged by her cheerfulness now.

"Wow," she looks at the dimly lit gray cement room as if it were something wonderful.

"We're at the end," I press my hand to the small of her back, leading her past row after row of empty lanes.

When we reach our lane, Declan places two gun cases on the wooden counter.

"The first rule of gun safety is actually two, but they are so critical, I'm calling them both rule one." she leans in, serious concentration etched into her face. "Always point the gun down when you're carrying it, handing it to someone, walking, whatever; if you aren't shooting, it's facing down. Then, equally important, your finger never touches the trigger unless you are ready to shoot."

After showing her how to load and unload, replace the clip, and slide back the bolt to put a bullet in the chamber, she's ready.

She takes the gun cautiously and steps toward the counter. I stand behind her with Declan. She rolls her small shoulders back and holds her arms outstretched, aiming the gun down the line.

The paper target looks much farther away than it normally does.

I step forward to encourage her, but the sharp, powerful banging of her shots starts. I stop, stunned until I hear the unmistakable clicking of an empty clip.

I expected a pause, a moment where she would need to

gather herself. She didn't hesitate, emptying the clip in only a few seconds. God, damn.

Declan makes an odd sound behind me, a surprised huff of air.

She pushes the button that pulls the mechanism forward, bringing her target toward us.

"Oh my God! Kane look!" She jumps up and down on her toes. The paper has two bullet holes, not on the human figure target but on the paper nonetheless.

"For the first time, that's better than I was expecting!" She laughs, and the arrhythmia is back.

Her laugh matches her smile, sweet and captivating. Her soft, full lips beaming over pearly white teeth. I have to force my gaze away from her mouth. Flashbacks of those same lips wrapped around my cock mere hours ago have my pants growing uncomfortable.

"A natural. I never had any doubts," I wink, and she rolls her eyes. Her gaze lingers for a moment over the front of my pants. Her body shivers, and she steps toward the counter, taking the second gun.

"Remember your stance," I call and watch her legs slide apart as she plants her feet.

Just as before, her small fingers pull the trigger in rapid succession, emptying the clip.

As the target slides toward us, she squeals. "I hit the target!"

A bullet hole pierces through what would probably be the wrist of the black silhouette. It's outside of the deadly target zone, but it's on the paper and touching the objective area.

Her arms snake around me carefully, making sure not to squeeze my ribs.

"I'm-" a chill runs down my spine as I'm interrupted by a shout from down the line.

Hanzo. Fuck.

She tenses in my arms.

"Reload the guns," I whisper to her as I press a kiss into her soft strawberry hair.

"What a coincidence running into you here!" His voice is like a grater against my ears.

"Yeah, a coincidence, I'm sure."

His fucking disgusting brother is standing behind him, openly watching Anaïs. His runny yellow eyes practically scream his repulsive thoughts. Clenching my hands by my sides is all I can do to keep from plucking his eyes from his skull.

I hope she is keeping her head down. I can't look at her. If I show too much concern, it will give me away.

"I'm sorry I missed you the other day. I was in the middle of a poker game, a million-dollar buy-in. I couldn't step away." He wheezes.

"I understand. I am grateful for your hospitality. I trust you received the token of my appreciation?"

"Ah, yes, you are too generous." Gray puffs of cigar smoke float around him and his brother. I hope it's not bothering her.

Haro leans forward, whispering into his brother's ear, as they both fix their gaze on Anaïs.

"We are having dinner with the section bosses tonight at my place. You should bring your lady friend." His mouth twists into a smile that makes me want to tear the skin from his bones. "We could use a bit of eye candy. Having a tight little bitch like that around will definitely improve."

He's testing me, I know this. It doesn't make it easier to control myself.

"Don't speak about her so disrespectfully. She is here as my guest, and I will not have you debasing her."

Hard as I try, I cannot hide the seething fury in my voice. My finger itches. If the next words out of his mouth aren't an apology he'll be eating a bullet.

"My apologies." His eyes are still watching her closely. "I look forward to tonight."

He waddles off, leaving a trail of pollution in the air.

I stand firm, waiting for them to be safely out of view before turning back to her. Her eyes are wide with panic.

"Do we have to go to that dinner?" She whispers with a shudder.

"Yes." I won't cower or show weakness. I'll bring her and they will all see the lengths I'm willing to go to to protect her. If any of them wants to challenge that, they will learn, tonight, just how stupid that would be.

CHAPTER 28

 naïs

KANE HAS BEEN EERILY quiet since our run-in with Hanzo.

As soon as he was sure they were gone, he yanked me out of the gun range and into the car so quickly I thought he was going to dislocate my shoulder. He didn't speak a single word in the car. I tried to ask him questions, but he only answered with irritated grunts.

I thought Hanzo's brother, all tall and skeletal, was creepy. As it turns out, Hanzo himself is no better. Short and round in comparison, but no less terrifying. They looked at me in a way that horrified me to my core. I don't want to go to this dinner. I don't ever want to see those men again, but I understand that we've been backed into a corner.

"Stop picking at your nails," Oksana swats my hand. "Close your eyes so I can do your eye makeup."

146

Jinx is napping in my lap. His warm, soft body snuggled across my legs is the only thing keeping me calm right now.

Oksana works quickly, swiping shadows and liners over my lids. I asked for something dramatic, hoping it would take her a long time to do. A desperate attempt to delay the inevitable.

"Ok, open so I can do the mascara," she hums.

I pick at my nails again. Mascara is the final touch, and then I'll be ready to go. Dressed, hair styled, makeup on.

"I don't want to go to this dinner," I whisper to her, fear gripping my vocal cords like a fist.

"I won't lie, I am not jealous that the invitation wasn't extended to me," she sighs, "but you have to go. They saw you, and now they're expecting you to be there. If he doesn't bring you, it will make him look weak, like he's afraid to have you near them."

"I know," I shutter.

A knock at the door makes me jump, startling Jinx, who jumps up in my lap before yawning and settling again. Until this moment, I never wished to be a dog. How simple and easy his life must be.

"Are you ready?" it's Declan.

"Yes," I open the door and follow him down the hall on shaky legs.

"Don't worry about Jiji," Oksana steps out behind us, "and for what it's worth, you look amazing!"

A nervous chuckle vibrates through my tight, nauseous throat.

As I step out of the hallway, Kane is standing by the elevator dressed in all black with his hair back. He looks incredibly handsome, even with the scowl carved into his face.

When he looks up to face me, his eyes travel from my

sky-high heels, up my legs, stopping at the top of my thighs, where the hem of my dress sits. For a moment, the anger disappears and the lust I'm growing accustomed to seeing flashes in his eyes.

The week I spent working at The Playground was a crash course in walking in heels so high they should be illegal. Right now though, my ankles and knees wobble.

When we step into the elevator, he lets out a deep gruff sigh.

I feel his fingers searching my side to take hold of my hand. He interlocks our hands and squeezes me tightly.

"You look beautiful," he whispers.

"Thank you, so do you," I whisper back, and Declan does a strange choking cough mixed with a laugh.

Kane shoots a murderous look, and he immediately swallows the sound, coughing inside his mouth.

"I'm not going to let anything happen to you tonight," Kane takes my chin in his hand as Declan pulls the car out of the underground garage. "I promise you, Anaïs, you will be safe."

"I know." My voice is squeaky and terrified, but I do mean it.

The drive to Hanzo's is so much faster than I remember. My heart pounds in my chest as the car rolls to a smooth stop in front of the door. The same doorman is standing outside waiting.

"Kane," I whisper as Declan gets out to open the doors. "I know this is horrible timing, but after this dinner, can we talk?"

His face pales slightly, and he adjusts the knot of his tie at his neck. "Of course," he clears his throat.

To get through this dinner, I'm planning to spend the entire time preparing a speech in my head. I'll figure out what I want to say to him. It's a win-win. I'll be distracted from this horrible dinner, and I won't fumble around with my thoughts later.

Kane's hand rests on the small of my back. As we walk inside, his pinky keeps sweeping down, sliding over my ass through the thin material of my dress.

The feeling of his hands on me is something I'll never get used to. It's so...stimulating.

We don't go up the back stairs this time. Instead, we're ushered through a large wooden sliding panel that takes us into a dimly lit room. Everyone else is already waiting.

A group of eleven is seated around a long, low table. Each of them watches us closely as we enter.

Kane places his hand on my neck, making my skin flush with goosebumps.

"Your shoes," he whispers as he slides his off.

"Ah!" Hanzo laughs loudly from the head of the table, "You made it!"

His creepy brother is seated beside him. Five men and four women are seated on cushions on the ground around the table.

I recognize some of the women from The Playground. I'm assuming that they are here in the same capacity that I am.

At least one of the men was a frequent patron there as well.

"Heard you ran into a bit of trouble the other day, Kane." A man that I've never seen before chuckles. His lips pull into a greasy smirk.

"I would hardly consider that trouble," Kane's voice is flat and emotionless. He's not taking the bait.

"Who is this lovely young thing?" The man goads him.

Kane tenses, but ignores the man and turns to Hanzo.

149

"You know I fucking hate small talk. Are we going to get down to business?" His voice is low and raspy, the softness I have grown to long for is nowhere in it. This is King Kane - boss Kane - not my Kane.

The wooden door slides open, and several women in strappy red lingerie enter carrying trays.

Hanzo gestures his hand over the table, and they quickly begin placing plates in front of everyone. Kane still has his hand on my neck. The feeling of his long, hard fingers gently digging into my skin makes me feel breathless.

Throughout the meal, I try to focus on the food and prepare myself for our talk. It's difficult though when Hanzo keeps yelling loudly and spewing food out of his mouth with his animated antics.

It seems like business is over when the man seated across from me speaks up again.

"I heard Zion was digging around about the attack. thinking it was Farly." He's talking to Kane, but he's looking at me.

Kane just hums, but his fingers tighten slightly.

Why won't this jerk let this go? It's like he wants Kane to be mad at him.

"Just makes me wonder what Farly must know," the man chuckles. "Why would he choose to attack now? Why not last month? Why not next month? Why right now?" He continues running his mouth with his heavy gaze on me.

"Is there something you know about the attack, Donley? By all means, please, do share."

"I don't know anything," he feigns sincerity.

"I should hope not because if you did, Zion might need to take a little trip down to that piece of shit, rodent-infested, come-bucket that you have the audacity to call a bar. You know, just to see if he could gather any information. I would hate to see your place of business shut down."

The smirk slips from the man's face, "that won't be necessary. I don't know anything."

Kane hums again, " We'll see." Now he's the one smirking.

One of the other men gasps and points his finger at me from across the table.

"Babydoll!" A big smile spreads across his face. "It's been bothering me all night! I knew I recognized you! I just couldn't place it! You're babydoll!"

"No fucking way!" One of the other men chimes in.

"Fuck me! Kane, where have you been hiding this one? When you're done with her, I would pay a pretty penny for a piece of that."

"What do you think, Babydoll?" He turns his attention to me. "When you're done playing with the king, how about you come and spend a little time with me? I'll pay you a good price, and I'll make sure that pretty little cunt is well taken care of."

Faster than I can even process it. Kane is moving both of his arms in sync. One hand moves up, pressing my head into his side while covering my ear to muffle the sound. The other hand whips a gun from under his jacket, sending a shot right between the man's eyes.

He jumps up, pulling me up with him. I close my eyes tight so that I don't have to see it but the smell of gunpowder and metallic blood hit me hard.

"Now hear this," Kane's voice is clear but low, "this woman is off-limits. This woman is mine. If any of you even think about pointing your peckers in her direction, I'll have them removed from your bodies and shoved down your fucking throats before I create another hole in your head."

I think I might be in shock because I don't even

remember leaving the building or getting into the car. It's as if I woke up as Declan was driving us down the dark streets.

When he pulls into the underground garage, Kane quickly scoops me into his lap. He makes a small, pained grunt as he lifts me into his arms and out of the car.

"I'm sorry, baby," he whispers before he presses a kiss to my temple, leaving his lips there as we ride up the elevator in silence.

When we reach the penthouse, he carries me through the foyer and starts to walk up the stairs.

"Are we not going to have our discussion?" My voice is small and shaky.

"You still want to talk to me?" He stops in the middle of the staircase.

"Yes."

CHAPTER 29

Anaïs

WE'RE SITTING in the middle of his huge bed, facing each other.

After the incident at Hanzo's, all the talking points I wanted to bring up and the thoughts I had organized and prepared have flown out of my head.

"Um, well." I fidget nervously, "I just have some questions." I clear my throat and try to sound confident.

"Anything, ask me anything." He's rock solid, as usual. His voice doesn't crack or waver. He's steady—completely sure and unshakable.

"I guess I just need some clarification." This feels so silly now after his declaration at the table. He made his feelings pretty clear.

"Ok," he nods, waiting for me to continue.

153

"You said that you want me to be your woman, what does that mean, really?"

"It means that I want you to be mine. My partner, my queen, my woman. If you want marriage and the title of wife, I would give it to you, but I don't care beyond the title of mine."

My heart is about to beat out of my chest, but he looks completely serene.

"If I'm yours, what does that make you to me?" I'm stuttering and stumbling over my words. It might have been a good idea to have this conversation tomorrow after the shock has worn off.

"I'm yours just the same way that you're mine. I'll be your partner. Your man?" His voice sounds a little unsure of that term at the end.

I'm still feeling a bit uncertain about what the expectations would be. Am I just supposed to sit in his house all the time?"

He must see my hesitation because he grabs my hands. "Anaïs, you would be the ruler of The Underworld, by my side, my equal, my partner, my better in every way."

"Your equal." The words don't feel right.

"Yes, I had that throne made for you and placed it beside me to show you where your place is and what I want from you. Everything I am, everything I have is yours. I am wholly devoted to you. You are the most beloved woman here, or anywhere."

The shock I felt earlier has returned. He's devoted to me?

"Will people know? Isn't it too dangerous?" My mind wanders back to Hanzo's sneering face at the shooting range. He looked so pleased, like he finally had something to leverage over Kane. I don't want to be the bait that people use against him. I don't want to be his weakness. I also can't go back to living my life hidden away like a prisoner.

"All of The Underworld will know," his voice is absolutely final, "there will not be a soul here below that does not know that you are mine and that you are the queen."

Leaning forward, he cups my face in his hands and hovers his lips above mine, "my queen."

The roughness in his voice sends a shiver down my spine. He's waiting, frozen before me, waiting for me to press our lips together or deny him.

It feels like standing at the edge of a cliff, solid ground too far down to even see. He's asking me to jump and promising to catch me, I just have to take a step. It's terrifying and exciting and everything in between.

I can't ignore the flutter in my heart. The only option is to force back the noise in my mind and let my heart take the lead.

When our lips touch, his calmness breaks. He pulls me up into his lap while kissing me so desperately that it makes me gasp. He doesn't waste the opportunity to slip his eager tongue into my mouth. The kiss is wet and hungry.

His fingers dig into my thighs, holding me onto his lap.

I want to be closer to him, so I scoot forward, hoping to press our chests together. Instead, my hips move up over his. He groans and looks down. The skirt of my dress is bunched up around my waist, and my little pink panties are hovering right over the zipper of his pants.

His hand comes up behind my head as he sits forward, dropping me down onto the mattress.

"Open your legs. I'm going to touch you." It's a statement, but he waits, looking for hesitation.

I drop my knees down, giving him the permission he's waiting for.

Instead of moving, he just stares down between my legs. It makes me feel so hot and wiggly. The way he looks at me is somehow unnerving and a boost of confidence. It's so vulnerable to have someone staring at your nakedness in your most private place. The look on his face is so appreciative? Awed? Full of lust? It's hard to feel self-conscious.

It feels cold and unpleasant between my legs. The air makes the wetness there uncomfortable. Finally, he moves, his hand coming up to tug the fabric down, leaving me completely exposed.

My body twitches when his fingers touch my skin, sliding through it. The more he moves, the harder it is for me to stay still. My body makes a wet, sticky sound against his fingers.

"You're so responsive, Anaïs," his voice is thicker than normal. "I love how wet you get for me."

"Oh my God!" I choke as he pushes one of his fingers inside of me suddenly.

His finger curls, and my hips start to move on their own. I can't stop them or keep them still.

With his free hand, he unbuttons his shirt, tearing the buttons open.

I'm not sure if it's his finger inside of me, the sight of his bare chest, the words he spoke, or a combination of all of it, but I suddenly feel bold. The same kind of unabashed boldness that led me to take him into my mouth.

Lifting my leg slowly, I carefully press my foot over the bulge in his pants. Not hard, just enough to feel it.

His hands stop their movements, and his head falls back. A low, rumbling sound in his chest vibrates all the way down against my foot.

I move my hips, hoping to feel his finger again, but he pulls it out, sucking it into his mouth.

"Kane." I'm a mess. My brain has turned to mush, and all I

can think about is him, his hands, his mouth, his — everything.

I want more of him, I want to touch him everywhere, to feel his skin on mine. I want it all.

When he unbuckles his pants and pulls his open shirt from his arms, I feel a sense of peace wash over me. I want to be right where I am. I want this with him at this exact moment. There are no doubts, no nerves, nothing but him and me.

When he pulls his underwear down, I can't help the whimper that slips past my lips. He is so big and hard. It was enough of a task to wrap my mouth around it. I'm a bit worried about being skewered by it.

"It will fit," a reassuring smile flashes over his face. He crawls over my body, nestling himself down between my legs. "We can go slow. We have all night."

CHAPTER 30

 naïs

EVERYTHING FEELS SO INTENSE. Each sweeping touch of his fingers, every soft kiss, every sigh, all add to the knot forming in my stomach.

I'm glad we're taking it slow. I don't want to rush through the moment, I don't want to forget a single touch or feeling. However, there comes a point when enough is enough.

He has pulled pleasure from me in every way I can imagine. His mouth and his fingers have licked, sucked, and rubbed me to a state of frenzied delirium.

If he brings his tongue down on me one more time, I might combust on the spot.

Grabbing his face in my hands, I pull him up, kissing his swollen lips. I can taste myself on his tongue. He hasn't let me touch him, not once. Each time I try, he pulls away, distracting me with kisses and his devilishly talented fingers.

158

"Kane, please," I'm pleading with him, and I feel absolutely no shame, "let me touch you."

He follows my gaze down his body to the thick, leaking length.

"You want to touch me?" His voice is teasing, but I can hear the strain, he can't hold out much longer.

"Yes," I shriek as he presses two of his fingers into me suddenly. Just as quickly as he pushed them in, he pulls them out.

"I can't wait to be inside of you," his forehead drops to mine.

I'm ready. I'm so wet, and every part of me aches and throbs. My muscles hurt from the constant tension of multiple orgasms. It doesn't seem to matter how many times he shatters the world around me, it's not enough. It's not the one thing that I really want.

"Please," if he doesn't do it soon, I'll die.

He shifts on the bed, reaching behind him into the side table. He sits back between my legs with a shiny square packet between his fingers.

I sit up quickly, watching as he rips it open. My thighs press together as he rolls it down his length.

He's been so calm, moving slowly. I feel like there are butterflies under my skin.

"Lay back, baby," He runs his fingers over my naked skin. All of our clothes have long since been stripped away and thrown to the side. Now, the only thing between us is a thin piece of rubber.

When he settles down between my legs again, I can feel him poking at my entrance. All of the anticipation that led us to this moment is finally about to be released.

My body trembles with nervous energy. Not fear but

with expectation. I just want him to do it already. I need relief from this pulsating rhythm between my legs.

"Look down," he groans as he nudges against me with a bit more pressure.

I let my eyes trail down his body to where he is nestled between my legs.

He rests his forehead on mine as we both look down, watching.

The pressure builds as he pushes forward, inward. I feel the tip of him enter me with a popping sensation.

"Oh God," I shudder, and he groans loudly.

"Jesus fuck," he chokes, "Relax, baby, I'll go slow; don't tense your body."

I take a breath and focus on relaxing the muscles between my legs.

When I'm relaxed, he presses in again. The pressure and stretching feeling are so intense that I tense again. I'm soaked, so friction isn't a problem. It's the tightness. It's like my body is just small enough that he has to force it.

He presses a soft kiss to the tip of my nose, his forehead still resting on mine, "It's ok, baby."

He lets me take a few deep breaths before continuing. Watching him disappear inside of me is so strange.

"Oh my fucking god," he groans loudly.

I feel completely full, like I can't possibly take any more of him in.

"It's not going to fit," I whimper and bite into my lip.

He slides out and brings his mouth to mine, "We can stop. Maybe we can try again another time or—"

"No!" I stop him. "I don't want to stop. Maybe just push it in."

He brings his mouth to mine, kissing me hard.

"Kane," he's not putting it back in. I think he's trying to distract me with kisses.

He watches my face, staring into my eyes for several seconds before moving back, pressing into me again.

"Just do it," I groan.

"Fuck," he moans, and his hips flex forward, tearing into me completely.

We both gasp. His from pleasure, mine from pain. I feel myself rippling and spasming around him. The ache throbbing as he stretches me past the point of comfort.

"Shit," he growls as he slides himself out, then back in slowly.

If he was one-inch longer, it wouldn't have fit. I'm so completely full, I think I can feel him in my stomach.

He moves slowly, his thumb circling my too tender and swollen bundle of nerves. The stinging ache and strong pressure are so strong that I can hardly focus on his fingers.

"Fuck, it feels like you were made for me," he groans in between nipping and sucking on my neck. "So fucking tight."

I definitely feel tight, like my body is trying to push him out of me.

When I whimper, he slows, pulling his face from my neck to look at me. His hips stop moving completely, and he focuses his attention on his fingers.

The pain starts to subside, and the overwhelming tightness in my stomach starts to build. He might not be moving, but he's inside of me. That knowledge, coupled with the tight circling of his thumb, has me coiling tighter and tighter, teetering on the edge.

He groans loudly and drops his sweaty forehead to mine.

"Fuck, that's it, baby, come."

My body reacts to his words with obedience. My legs

shake around his waist, and broken sobs pour from my lips. I can feel him inside of me, my body tensing around him.

With my core still pulsating, he starts to move again, slowly, dragging himself through my spasming, sore body.

With the pain almost gone now, I can focus on his face and body, on what is happening deep between my legs.

I can feel every ridge, the thick tip rubbing my walls as he moves.

His face is etched in bliss. The part in his soft lips lets out grunts and sighs and little moans in between swear words. His eyes move between holding my gaze and looking down at where we come together. He looks so handsome. Even now, with our bodies joined together, I blush if I stare at him too long.

With hooded eyes, he watches his length, slick and wet, disappearing into me.

A deep, low rumbling sound in his chest grabs my attention. It's the same sound he made before he came before.

"Oh-fuck," he grits out, and his hips roll against mine.

I gasp, and tears prick my eyes. I can feel him—really feel him. He pulses inside of me, pleasure and relief washing over his face.

I'm his woman. He is devoted to me, only. This man between my legs put me on a throne beside him. His equal. His Queen. It sounds too good to be true, but he's never given me a reason to doubt him.

I feel so close to him—closer than I've ever felt to anyone. He was so gentle. He's always gentle. Any time he touches me, there is a sweetness, a protectiveness, making sure I'm comfortable.

"Why are you crying?" He pulls out of me slowly and removes the condom before lying beside me.

"I don't know. I just feel emotional."

He chuckles and kisses the palm of my hand, "I understand."

When I sit up next to his relaxed body, my hand comes down to a wet stain on the dark sheets. The tips of my fingers are red. I quickly close my fist and put my hand in my lap. I don't want Kane to see.

"Anaïs," his voice is soft, "you don't need to be embarrassed."

My cheeks are red, and I try to keep my head down, but he hooks his finger under my chin.

"Come here," he whispers softly as he stands and lifts me from the bed.

"Where are we going?"

"The bathroom, I'm going clean you up."

When he set me down on the floor, the muscles in my thighs and between my legs ache. The tenderness makes me wince.

Trying to distract myself, I look around the dark bathroom. He starts the water to fill the huge black bathtub.

"Do you like this?" He holds out a jar filled with an iridescent milky liquid.

I sniff it. I really like it. It's soft and floral. It reminds me of the lotion Oksana gave me.

He chuckles at my smile and enthusiastic nod before dumping it into the running water.

I shift on my feet, ready to be engulfed in the warm water. The soreness seems to be growing.

When he drops his knees in front of me, I try to take a step back, but he holds my hip and gently taps my knees.

"Open your legs."

It's ridiculous considering everything that we've just done, but I am embarrassed and I don't want to.

"Anaïs," his voice is gentle and coaxing, "open."

Parting my legs gently, he brings a wet cloth up and carefully rubs the apex of my thighs and over my tender skin. When I'm sufficiently clean, he leans forward, pressing kisses to each thigh and just below my belly button.

"Get in," he kisses my stomach again.

CHAPTER 31

 ane

"Good morning!" Loud screaming from outside of the room startles me awake. "Wake the fuck up!" It's Zion. Yelling as loud as he possibly can.

Anaïs pulls the sheet over her head and curls into my body. Momentary relief fills me that it isn't some ill-intentioned enemy.

The relief quickly fades to irritation. With a groan, I pull her closer to me. "I'm going to fucking kill him."

"Yo!" He's pounding on the door, "Wake up, birthday boy!"

She gasps and wiggles out of my grasp, sitting up.

"Is today your birthday?" Her sweet voice calms the anger Zion always seems to trigger.

With my eyes still closed, I reach out, feeling around the bed for her.

"Come back here."

"No! Answer me! Is it your birthday?" She swats at my hand.

Before I can respond, Zion starts pounding again. "Get the fuck up, Kane! I told you I wasn't going to let you get out of this!"

"What is he talking about?"

Fuck.

"He's throwing me a birthday party." I catch her arm and pull her back to my chest.

Turning my head toward the door, I yell out, "A birthday party tonight. There is absolutely no reason for your annoying ass to be here right now!"

"I'm just making sure you're coming!" Zion laughs. He really enjoys pissing me off.

"You're having a birthday party?" She runs the tips of her fingers over my stomach.

"Do you want to go?"

"I've never been to a party," she presses her fingers down, letting her whole hand run over my skin.

Oh, fuck me.

My muscles tense, and my already hard cock twitches.

Spinning us in the bed I cage her beneath my body. Her hair is sprawled out over my pillow, her lips are still swollen from last night, and her naked body is beneath mine.

"We'll be there; go the fuck away," I yell toward the door before pressing my lips against hers.

I can't get enough of her. It's almost unbearable now that I've felt her. Now that I know how it feels to be buried inside of her, I can't think of anything else.

Jesus Christ. She was so warm. Warm and soft and fucking tight. Pressing myself into her was the single greatest thing I've ever done in my life.

"Kane," she moans into my mouth.

Fuck, I love it when she does that.

"Yeah, baby," I let my hand slide down her body, searching for the slick wetness between her legs that makes my head explode.

"Are we going to talk about last night?"

I let out a whiny groan like a pouty child.

"What's to talk about?" That motherfucker was out of line, so I blew his brains out. Word travels fast around here. No one will speak to her like that again. They might whisper it in hushed tones in secret, far away from me, but they'll never be stupid enough to do it in my presence.

"You killed a man for saying things that, in all honesty, are fairly tame. The men at The Playground would say much harsher things to all the girls."

"I don't care about all the girls. Only you. No one will ever disrespect you like that again."

"Well, first of all, I care about the girls. Second, you can't just kill people because they say something you don't like." She quirks her brow at me, and the small, sassy gesture makes my cock ache.

"Actually," I thrust myself against her, "I absolutely can kill someone for saying something I don't like. It's one of the perks of my position."

She moans and arches her head off the bed.

"Are you too sore?"

"No," she's already breathless. Her hands run through my hair, and I press my face down into her neck. Goosebumps erupting over my skin as she works her fingers through. I don't know what it is about this that I like so much. It makes me feel warm everywhere.

"Are you sure?" I pull myself up and kiss her softly, from her neck to just below her stomach.

She only hums and arches toward me. The sounds she makes fuck me all the way up. Maybe everything she does has an effect.

Watching her face, I press my mouth to her opening, kissing her softly on her tender skin. With gentle licks and kisses, I lap at her, making sure to leave nothing unattended. I know that she likes it when I move my tongue quickly, but today I'm taking my time, careful to be gentle to the sensitive place that gave me so much pleasure last night.

I want to cherish it, to show it proper love.

Even with my leisurely movements, I feel her pleasure building. Her breathing is shallow and rapid. Her legs tremble. Even from the outside, I can feel her body starting to clench.

Precum drips from my cock at the thought of how tight her pussy would be right now if I were inside her.

When she came last night, the pressure nearly brought me to tears.

"Oh, Kane," she sighs, her fluttering voice wrapping around me.

When she gasps, I lick slightly faster, tasting the sweet, earthy flavor of her wetness as she comes on my eager tongue.

I pull myself up, kissing a trail of wet kisses up her body.

"Happy birthday to me," I grin at her sweet, giggling laughter.

Her fingers run over my chest, and she kisses and sucks my neck.

"Fuck, that feels so good." Why does everything she does to me feel like this?

Her hands move lower, over my abdomen, teasing.

"Can we have sex again?" She asks with shyness in her tone. As if she's not sure I'll want to.

Happy birthday to me, indeed.

Just as I reach for a condom, the loud banging on my door resumes.

"Kane, it's actually important this time, get the fuck out here." The seriousness in his voice makes my skin prick.

What I wish for my birthday is to beat the shit out of my brother.

"Fuck! If this isn't really important, I'm going to kill you!" I tear myself away from her.

CHAPTER 32

 naïs

"COME ON, Oksana, none of this is helpful!"

She laughs and tugs Jiji's toy from his mouth.

I need to get Kane a birthday gift, but I don't have any money or any time. The party is tonight! All of her suggestions have been less than helpful.

-Be naked in his bed.

-Edible lingerie.

-Birthday cake frosted lady parts.

None of these things seem special enough. I want to give him something amazing—something that will surprise him. He already has everything.

"You could finally have sex with him?" She's actually serious about this one.

I feel red flames sweep over my cheeks.

"Oh my fucking god!" She jumps up, "You fucked him!"

Jiji drops his toy, momentarily distracted by her sudden screaming.

"No! We didn't do that! " I'm a liar, I'm a liar, I'm a liar.

"Holy shit," her eyes are wide, "you fucked the devil. Wow. How was it?"

She sits beside me again, crossing her legs and staring at me, waiting for details that I won't be sharing.

"Oksana, focus! Birthday gifts, please! I don't know when he'll be back. I need to figure something out!" I hope she allows this change of subject. I can't talk about it. It's too special and private.

"You're not going to tell me about it?" She sighs, "Some friend!" She pouts for a second. "At least tell me, is he big? Zion is huge, and Kane has this, I don't know. An energy. He's got to be packing something massive."

"How do you know about Zion?" I hope she doesn't realize that I changed the subject and ignored her question.

"Girl, remember when I told you about his girls? I was one of them," she laughs. "I was his fuck of the week once upon a time."

I'm completely shocked. How is she laughing about this? If Kane dismissed me after a week, I would be heartbroken.

"It didn't hurt your feelings?" My heart aches thinking of her sadness.

"What? Girl, no. The only thing he hurt was my vag with his monstrous cock."

We're both laughing when she suddenly gasps and grabs my arm.

"Oh my god, Anaïs, dance for him!"

"What?"

"I'm serious! You have some really great lingerie that you never got to use. Take the stage, Babydoll! Give him a sexy show for his birthday!"

Flop sweat, nerves, and anxiety. I can't do that! Can I? Would he like that?

I'm torn. His brother owns the club, and he obviously visits on occasion. I get the feeling he would be upset by others looking at me. Then again, he obviously liked my dance on the night we met.

"Men love that shit, you know that!" She nudges my shoulder.

He told me he would be devoted to me, does that mean he won't go watch other dancers? Will he miss it? Is that something he enjoys?

Being his woman means acclimating to his world. The Playground is a big part of his world.

I don't know what to do. It might be a wonderful idea, or it could be the worst thing I've ever heard.

"I don't know if it's a good idea, he can be kind of possessive." The memory of last nights events is still too fresh in my mind.

"You're going to be dancing for him though, and it's a VIP event, the club is going to be closed to everyone but guests." She jumps up and starts walking toward the stairs. "Let's go look through your closet. Even if you don't dance, we need to know what you're working with outfit-wise."

"Oh, um… I'm not upstairs anymore. My things were moved this morning."

She stops midstep and turns to face me, her mouth hanging open. "Bitch, did he move you into his bedroom?"

I shrug my shoulders and nod.

"Well, there's no way in all of The Underworld I'm going in there! You're going to have to bring some options out for me to look at."

When I'm alone in the closet, looking through my dresses, my eyes keep wandering back to the shelves with my lingerie displayed on them. I wonder if he would like that. I have nothing else to give him. He would definitely be surprised.

I wonder if he would like it...

The thought of doing it for him makes me feel kind of... fluttery. Last time I danced, I kept my eyes down and never looked at the crowd. I would like to see him, to see his face. After last night, I can understand why people become obsessed with sex. The look on his face is enough to make me do almost anything to see it again.

Grabbing a dress, I leave the closet quickly. This is the dress I want to wear. I hope she likes it.

It's short, white, and shimmery. Kane had my shopper buy a lot of white. I'm guessing he likes it even though he's always in black.

I hardly make it out the door before Oksana is clapping.

"Yes! That's the one! Have you tried it on yet? You should try it on for good measure, but I think it's perfect!"

A warm, comforting feeling settles in my chest. I always wanted a friend. A person who I could spend time doing these things—talking, laughing, and joking. Now I have two people.

Though Kane still makes me feel flutters of nervousness.

"I think I'm going to do the dance," I chew my lip nervously.

"Yes!" She jumps up, "What lingerie are you going to wear? We should start your hair and makeup. With that dress, I'm thinking total vampy sex kitten. Smokey eye, big hair...."

I'm so anxious that I hardly hear her. I just nod in agreement with her suggestions.

Hours of primping take up the rest of the day. Washing,

waxing, oils and perfumes, makeup, nail polish, and hair products. By the time we're actually ready, I'm exhausted.

After securing the clasp on my heels, I stand in front of the mirror.

I don't look like myself. The woman standing before me looks sexy. Confident even. Not like me at all.

"Kane is going to lose his shit," she bumps her hip into mine.

As if on cue, the elevator dings downstairs.

He's back!

Running carefully in my shoes, with Jiji on my heels, I make my way to the stairs.

The sight of him takes my breath away. His hair is disheveled, and he's not wearing his jacket. The sleeves of his button-down are rolled up over his tan arms. I might need to change my panties before we leave.

We make eye contact, and for a moment it's like there isn't anyone else in the room.

"Jesus Christ," he growls, taking the stairs two at a time, "you look fucking gorgeous."

I'm pulled into him as he brings his face into my neck.

"Can we please skip this party?" He begs against my ear.

"No, go get dressed." It takes all of my self-control not to agree to stay home in bed.

Who am I?

CHAPTER 33

 ane

IT LOOKS like I'll be wearing my jacket all night in an attempt to cover this fucking erection.

After we left the apartment this morning, everything went to absolute shit. Today has been a fucking nightmare.

Then, there she is.

Radiant as the sun.

All the bullshit just melts away. Tomorrow is going to be a hell of a day, but for now, it's just her, in that fucking dress, sitting beside me.

Something is off though. Every time I ask, she mumbles about being fine, but I can see it. As Dec stops the car in front of the club, I have to try again. This will be the last time we'll have a quiet place to talk for a while.

"Anaïs?" I press a kiss to her palm. "You're so tense. What's the matter?"

"Nothing," her smile gives her away. She's nervous.

"Are you afraid that something will happen tonight?" She's probably scared I'm going to kill someone.

Which is valid.

"No." There is no confidence behind her answer.

"Listen, I want you to have fun tonight. I'll be on my best behavior, I promise. There will be all manner of immorality and wickedness at our disposal, enjoy yourself." I bring my hand to her thigh, just resting it there. With my other arm, I lock the door.

Her breath catches, a little gasp that feels like a jolt of electricity into my already aching cock.

Letting my fingertips slide slowly upward, I feel her thighs tense and press together.

The door clicks, and Dec tries to open it for us from the outside.

"Go!" I growl.

The sound immediately stops, and he walks away from the car, waiting by the door to The Playground with the bouncers.

"Kane, they'll see us." She's breathless, and I haven't even touched her.

"The window tint is so dark they can't see inside, open your legs." I'm practically drooling. If she asked, I would get down on my knees in front of everyone here and beg her.

There are several things I would do on my knees in front of everyone.

She hesitates for a moment before I feel her tense thighs part slightly.

I let my fingers graze her until I'm met with the warm, wet stripe of fabric.

She pinches her eyes closed and lets her head fall back against the headrest.

"Fuck," I grit my teeth, "I ache for you, all the time."

Pushing my fingers further, I move under the material to feel her skin. She whimpers, and her legs separate further.

"Anaïs, I need you to be honest with me, do you really want to go to this party?"

Her eyes flutter open. "I do, but it's your birthday. If you would rather go, we can."

"No, let's go. My cock will still be hard when we get home. We can enjoy the party." I pull my hand out from under her dress.

A tiny smile pulls at her lips.

Fuck. This is going to be a long night.

Declan jogs toward the car when we step out. I grab his arm as he passes me, speaking quietly, "Have the car ready when I call."

"Yes, Sir."

The bouncer holds the door open, his eyes drifting quickly over her body as we walk past.

I told her I would be on my best behavior tonight.

When we walk inside, the club is chaotic.

Her hand grips mine tightly as she looks around. Zion has really outdone himself.

Sodom and Gomorrah.

We stop walking, just standing by the bar while she takes everything in. Each of the seven deadly sins is represented here at least once.

Lust in particular.

The lights have been changed to red and purple, everything is bathed in the eerie glow. A row of ten dancers is on the stage wearing only glowing body paint.

There is a fire breather on one end of the stage and a contortionist on the other.

A group of five people has already begun having sex on one of the loungers with more than a few spectators.

A dominatrix wearing nothing but thigh-high boots is working a scene with a man strapped to a play table. He's face down with his cock hanging through a glory hole.

Anaïs quickly looks away. If the lights weren't so harsh, I'm sure I'd see a blush.

A huge buffet of decadent food is set up on one side of the room.

Her eyes dance curiously over everything. This is a safe area, nothing wild or uncomfortable here. She looks calmer. Food is good, food is nonthreatening. Food isn't leaking bodily fluids all over the lounge...

"Want a drink?" I lean down, taking in the smell of her hair.

"Sure," she smiles, but she's not confident.

One of Zion's parties might not have been the right choice for her first party.

"The guest of honor has arrived!" Zion yells as he jumps over the bar. "What the fuck, Kane? The dress code was leather, lace, or latex!"

Anaïs' eyes shoot to mine.

"Fuck off, you knew I wasn't about to wear that." I look at his leather pants.

"You're no fun!" He runs his hands over his bare chest and starts dancing a little bit and smiling at Anaïs.

Quickly pulling her away, I move to the other end of the bar to get our drinks.

"Why didn't you tell me there was a dress code?" She looks upset as she scans the room, studying everyone's clothes.

"I wanted you to wear what you want, and I'm glad you did, you look stunning."

When she doesn't respond, I look down, and she's mouthing words and staring across the room.

Oksana is sitting on Zion's lap now. "I didn't know!" She scrunches up her face and points to her dress, which is also not within his stupid wardrobe requirements.

Her shoulders relax some.

"Anaïs," her big eyes look up at me, "relax, baby, you can wear whatever you want."

I turn to order the drinks. While I'm talking to the bartender, I feel her body tuck in closer to mine. When I turn to hand her the glass, she's zoned out. Following her gaze toward a large booth in the back, I feel her tense.

The group at the table is passing around a small mirror, snorting lines through a rolled-up dollar bill.

"What drug is that?" She leans up on her toes to ask.

"Cocaine."

"And that?" She points toward a large punch bowl full of pills.

"Different things, Xanax, oxy, ecstasy..."

When someone pulls out syringes, she quickly looks away, moving her gaze toward the stage.

The best booth in the house has been reserved for me. At the end of the catwalk.

"Would you like to sit?"

She nods and squeezes my hand.

Sliding into the booth beside her, I notice her fingers, knotted together in her lap.

"Baby, are you ok? We can leave." The tension in her shoulders is bothering me. I want her to enjoy herself.

"No, this is your birthday party. We can stay, it's just different than what I was expecting." She bites her lip as her eyes flick back and forth to all of the chaos again.

"More debauchery?"

"Yes," she giggles, "there are just so many things to look at." Her breath catches as she stops her gaze on the dominatrix.

Oh, fucking hell, she looks interested.

She watches as the man begs his mistress to keep slapping him with a crop.

"Doesn't that hurt?" She leans in close to my chest.

"Yes, but he likes it. He wants her to do it." My pants are uncomfortably tight. Watching her see these things for the first time —watching her period —it's getting to me.

Looking around, I try to assess if I could reasonably make her come here without anyone noticing. The whole party is busy with their own depravity, they probably won't notice mine.

Resting my hand on her knee, I can feel her breathing change immediately.

Just as I attempt to slide my hand up, I stop, rage filling me to the point of murderous violence.

"Kane Azrael, happy birthday!"

This mother fucker has some fucking nerve!

CHAPTER 34

 naïs

I'M FROZEN with his hand on my knee, his fingers biting into my skin. I don't know who this is, but by Kane's reaction, I know we don't want him here.

"May I sit?" He smiles at Kane, who still hasn't spoken a word.

I feel his hand twitch against my leg.

"Farly," Kane's voice is more like a rumbling growl. I bite back a gasp. I need to be stoic, unemotional, more like Kane. I can't be caught off guard, weak.

This is Cohen Farly? What is he doing here?

He is very handsome. Not like Kane—it's different. He looks like a wolf in sheep's clothing. His youthful face and careless hair hide something sinister underneath. I can see it glowing behind his eyes. There is venom behind his perfect smile.

181

He slides into the booth with us, his large entourage of very imposing men, gathering around in a way that makes me feel like circled prey.

I don't understand the dynamic here. It's obvious that Farly feels some sense of safety. Whether it's false security or not, I can't tell. From what I've been told, he's untouchable, but so is Kane.

"Anaïs," he extends his hand to me. "It's so lovely to meet you finally. I am Cohen Farly."

Kane's facial expression doesn't change, but his fingers start to press painfully into my skin. How does he already know my name? The thought of my name passing from mouth to mouth in the dark corners of The Underworld is unnerving.

"Hello," I clear my throat.

"What do you want, Farly?" Kane's voice is eerily calm.

"I wanted to come by and invite you to the opening of my bar and gambling hall."

"Finally got that little venture off the ground, did you?" Kane raises an eyebrow. There is something going on here—a history that I'm not privy to.

"Yeah, you know, I had to grease a few wheels, but eventually it fell into place, it just took longer than I expected." If he's irritated, I can't tell.

"When is the opening?" Kane looks so bored that he might actually fall asleep.

"Next weekend, I would love to see you both there."

Kane hums, "We'll see if we can find the time."

"Heavy is the head that wears the crown, I get it, you're busy." A slick smile spreads over his face. "You know, if you can't come, it would be my absolute pleasure to host your Queen for the evening."

"I don't think so." I surprise the whole table, including

myself. He's trying to provoke him, and I don't like it. I don't understand these people. Kane has shown himself. He doesn't have patience for people, yet they continue to test him anyway. It must be some kind of death wish.

Kane chuckles, "The Queen has spoken."

For the first time since Farly sat down, Kane's expression has changed. He looks proud? Maybe? His fingers slide up my thigh, his thumb rubbing slowly over my flaming skin.

God. Just one touch and I'm melting into a puddle. This is not the time to be thinking of such things, but his hands make me weak.

"Well, I hope you can make it. It really will be a spectacular event, it might even give Zion a run for his money." He smiles, but it's not the same as before. It's not easygoing or arrogant like before. In fact, he looks angry.

When he slides out of the booth, nodding curtly in my direction, it's confirmed.

"I think you offended him," Kane chuckles and pulls me out of the seat into his lap. "Fuck, the things I want to do to you right now." He flexes his hips up, pressing himself up against me.

"Kane," my mind is a mess. His body below mine makes it difficult to think of anything else, but I want to know what just happened.

"How did he know my name?"

"I told you word spreads fast, baby. You're the talk of the town," he grunts and presses his hips up again.

"What happened this morning? Why did you have to rush off?"

"Umm, fuck," for the first time, he seems flustered. "Zion's goon squad arrested a few of Farly's guys. It was a legit arrest for assault, but now that we have them, we're going to get information out of them about the attack, about his plans."

"Why would he come here if he had you ambushed?" I roll my hips slightly, and his eyes roll back.

"Jesus Christ, baby, are you trying to kill me?" He sucks below my ear for a moment before groaning. "I would assume it's to keep up appearances. An innocent man wouldn't shy away."

That makes sense.

"Does that answer your questions? Can I take you somewhere else now? Have you had enough of this party? Please, baby."

Oh God, he's begging. I feel lightheaded.

He feels so hard against my wet panties that I'm sure he's going to burst through his zipper at any moment.

"K-Kane, oh my... God." My heartbeat is pounding between my legs.

He starts to slide around the booth, moving around the table to stand with me still in his arms.

Oh, no. Zion and Oksana are walking toward us.

My plan was to sneak away and forget the dance altogether.

"I'm afraid we're here to steal your woman," Zion says with a mischievous smile. Oksana said she would tell him everything so he would know my song. I also asked for specific lighting to be set.

"Get fucked," his face is full of irritation. "She isn't going anywhere with you!"

"Actually," I swallow nervously, "I have a surprise for you so, I do need to go with them."

He looks completely baffled.

"Where are you going?" he leans in to ask quietly into my ear.

"Don't worry, Oksana will be with me, and I'll be back soon, ten minutes, tops."

He bites into his lip, looking into my eyes. I can see his hesitation to let me out of his sight.

"Please, be careful," he sighs, releasing his tight grip on my hips.

"Kane, we aren't going to feed her to wild dogs, fuckin' relax, man." Zion laughs, but my eyes widen. Great, just what I need—that visual put in his head. Now he's never going to let me go.

Pressing a fast kiss against his tight-set mouth, I jump up from his lap before he can stop me.

Just before I disappear behind the bar, I turn and blow him a quick kiss. He clutches his heart with a boyish grin on his face. I still see the nervousness etched into his features but the smile makes my heart stop for a beat.

I hope he likes this.

CHAPTER 35

 naïs

I CAN HEAR Zion announcing a "special surprise for the birthday boy."

I suddenly wish I had grabbed another drink. After that tense moment with Cohen Farly and Kane's deep, raspy voice asking me to leave with him, I'm feeling more on edge. I know Zion's security had most of the party leave but there are still enough people here to make me nauseous.

Adjusting my lingerie one more time, I wait behind the curtain. This is for Kane - for his birthday. I can do this.

"Go get 'em," Oksana winks as the first blazing guitar riff of my song starts.

Here goes nothing.

As I step out onto the stage, the soft, pastel disco light swirls all around me. The rapid beating of my heart in my ears drowns out the music as I take a step forward.

It's as if fog rolled into the room, making everything hazy and out of focus. Everything except him.

He's all I see.

Walking the length of the stage straight toward him, I feel simultaneously calm and completely frantic.

His eyes are dark, and his jaw is clenched tight. I watch his chest rise and fall quickly, in time with mine. Forcing my eyes closed, I let the rhythm of the music take over. Flashes of him play like recordings in my mind. His eyes. His chest. His hands. His tongue.

Memory is a funny thing. It's like I can feel him physically. As I turn and sway, his skin lingers on mine. I can smell him around me, clean and strong. Each movement of my body is a response—a reaction to his movements in my mind.

This song is very different from my last one. This is loud and aggressive. The beat makes me feel powerful, like I actually belong here, like I'm a woman. Like I'm Kane Azraels woman.

Right now, on this stage, in these thigh-high boots, I am affecting the most feared man in The Underworld.

In a brief flash of weakness, I glance up at him. He standing at the end of the stage, his arms outstretched, holding him up against it. His head is tucked down, but his eyes are on me, following my every move.

He is a very large man; he always looks imposing, but right now, he could make me do anything.

His shoulders are tense, and every muscle looks ready to strike out. With his eyes following me across the stage, I spin slowly on my feet, letting my body come to a stop just an arm's length from him.

As the last note is played and the final lyric is sung, the whole room is silent.

"Get the fuck out," his voice is low and rumbling. Each word is punctuated with authority.

In a sudden burst of chaos, everyone scrambles, leaving as quickly as they can in whatever state they are in. No one stops to set down a glass or collect their belongings. It's a mass exodus. It's pandemonium. People are tripping over their own feet and knocking one another out of the way to ensure they aren't the last one out the door.

It only takes a moment for us to be completely alone.

Cigarettes are burning in ashtrays, and a sink behind the bar is running water.

He hasn't moved aside from the ragged breaths he's taking.

I don't know what to do.

When he lifts his head, his eyes burn into my exposed skin. In a fluid, quick motion, he leaps upward, his hands planted on the stage, his legs coming up. Standing slowly, he walks toward me, removing his jacket as he approaches.

"Anaïs," the sound of his voice rumbles in my chest and makes anticipation swirl in my stomach.

He might be mad, but there is much more than anger swirling in his eyes.

His lips and his hands reach me at the same time. A crushing kiss and his fingers biting into the skin under my thighs. He holds me against him, rubbing me up and down over the front of his pants.

I want to ask if he's angry at me or if he liked the dance, but I can't even breathe, let alone speak. His mouth is on mine with bruising force, clashing teeth, searching tongues, wet and messy.

My heart leaps to my throat at the sensation of falling as he drops down, first to his knees before laying me on my back on the stage.

Holding himself up with one hand, he lets the other roam my body, over my chest, down my stomach, into my panties.

A rough groan tears through him, rumbling in his chest as his fingers run through the slickness between my legs. He jerks his hand back, moving it to his belt. He's impatient, yanking and pulling at his clothes that aren't cooperating.

"Here," I reach my trembling hands out, gently undoing his belt and his button.

When he pulls his pants down, his hard length slaps against my stomach.

His fingers come up, gently tracing over one of the small white flowers embroidered on my black panties.

"What I'm about to do to you will not be gentle," his voice is strained, "I'm going to fuck you, Anaïs, do you understand?"

"Y-Yes," I meet his burning gaze. I want to ask a million questions, cower in fear, and moan at the sight of him, but I can't. He looks unhinged. The calm demeanor, the gentleness I've grown accustomed to, is gone, replaced with primal need, with lust. Deep down, I still trust that he won't hurt me, even in this state.

His fingers grip my panties tight, and he tears them away from my body with a stinging snap of the fabric.

The swollen tip slides against my skin before pushing into me hard.

The deep, growling sound of relief that falls from his lips makes my stomach clench. He slides out and slams forward quickly, my body not having any time to adjust at all. A whimpering, moan, pain mixed with pleasure sneaks past my lips before I bite down.

"My cock has been aching for you all night," he grits out through clenched teeth. "Fuck, I missed you, baby."

In an incomprehensible way, I know exactly what he

means. I missed him too. I missed this close, vulnerable, open feeling that I've only felt with him.

My nails dig into his shoulders as I cling to him. My emotions feel so heavy that I need to physically hold him to keep myself from bursting into tears.

"Angel, angel, angel," he chants under his breath, soft kisses peppering my neck and chest. His mouth doesn't match the roughness of his hips.

"Kane, please," I'm not even sure what I'm begging for. More? Less?

He angles his hips up and slams into me, hitting me so deeply that my back arches off the stage, and I scream into his mouth. Our wet skin slapping together and our panting breaths echo in the empty club.

My eyes roll back, and I feel myself starting to tighten, a ball of pleasure forming in my stomach.

"No," he grunts and pulls out, "don't come yet."

I gasp at the sudden emptiness, at the complete loss of the feeling that was building.

"Turn around. Get up on your knees." He sits back, waiting for me. "I want your ass up, in the air."

My body shudders as I turn, pushing myself up onto my knees. This position is so vulnerable. I can't see him, but he can see everything. I'm completely exposed to him.

Surrendering to the feeling —to the fear— I close my eyes and wait.

CHAPTER 36

 ane

HER BODY SHAKES and trembles as I run my fingers through her dripping wet pussy. Leaning further back on my heels, I stare at the soft, glistening skin.

"Drop your face down." I want her ass up in the air.

She brings her face down slowly, cautiously.

The view from here is spectacular. Everything perfectly displayed for me. Each time I see her, my mind can't wrap itself around how fucking beautiful she is or how amazing she feels.

"Do you have any idea how much trouble you're in?" I groan, sinking into her. My cock slides through her hot cunt.

She's so fucking tight and slippery.

I can't believe she got on stage in this tiny fucking outfit and danced in front of all of those people. I rock my hips back and slam into her.

Her knees slip, and she struggles to keep herself steady. I want her to scream, to cry out, to fucking beg me to let her come. I'm still deciding if I'm going to or not.

I want to pluck the eyeballs from every person who saw her tonight. I also feel a strange pride stirring in my stomach. She is so perfect. So soft and pure, and mine. The room was captivated. I'm not sure a single person took a breath while she swayed on the stage. Everyone was in awe of my woman.

Her sexy ass and thick thighs are at odds with her innocence and sweetness.

When Zion started announcing her, I thought it was a joke. She's usually so timid, I never believed that she would willingly take the stage.

Fuck. The lights danced over her skin, the way her hips rolled with the music.

I drill into her, pushing my cock as deep as I can.

Her moans and whimpers are muffled, but I can feel her body tensing. Grabbing her hips, I pull her back, slamming her back as I press forward.

"You're mine."

"Yes," she almost screams. "Yours. Please."

I slow my hips, rolling into her gently. Not yet, baby.

"K-Kane, please," her thighs shake as she arches into me, desperate for relief.

"What do you need, baby?"

"I... I need... please," she's flustered, choking on moans.

I pull out of her, punishing myself as much as her. Her small fist slams onto the stage as her head whips around to look at me. Her sweet face is full of pent-up frustrations.

"Kane!" Her cheeks are flushed, and strands of hair are stuck to her damp face and neck.

Gripping her hips, I slam back into her. The scream that erupts from her lips sets my blood on fire.

"Oh my God," she moans, her hands moving frantically like she's searching for something to grip.

"Put your hands behind your back," I grunt, waiting for her.

She hesitates but obeys, clasping her hands on the small of her back. With one hand, I hold them there, pressed against her. The other hand grips her hip, holding her in place.

Her thighs and ass shake every time I slam forward, the force of my hips making her body jerk forward.

She tenses again, pulsating around me.

"Oh, Kane, I'm-" She cries out just as I still.

"Did I say you could come?"

She lets out a shaky, frustrated breath, "No, but..."

"Do you want to come?"

"Yes, please, Kane." The desperation in her voice makes me twitch.

"Beg for it."

Her breath catches, and for a moment she's silent.

"Kane, please," she whimpers as I circle my hips slowly, building little by little.

I feel her tensing again, and I can't stop this time. I don't have the restraint to pull out now.

"Please, please, I'm sorry about the dance, please, let me come," her whole body shakes as she cries out.

The pressure of her, the way she's squeezing me—it's too much. It's too tight. She's too warm.

"Anaïs, holy fuck, come now, come with me," I can't fucking think straight. Her name rolls off my tongue—a poem, a song, a prayer.

Releasing her arms, my body slumps over hers. Rolling onto my back, I try to grab her, but she pulls away.

"You're mad at me?" Her voice is small.

193

"Yes. no. I'm not mad, I feel..." I don't know how I feel.

"Then what? You were so rough, which is fine," she blushes, "but you-"

"Wouldn't let you come?" I finish for her, and she blushes again.

"Why?" Her voice is soft.

"You're mine."

"Yes," she nods her head.

"And I didn't shoot anyone."

A small smile pulls at her lips. "No, you didn't." She shifts her body around, sitting on her knees in front of me. "You didn't like the dance?"

"I fucking loved the dance, it just took me by surprise."

"I don't understand. If you loved it, why are you mad? Why did you make me beg? That felt like I was being punished..." Her brows are furrowed.

I'm as confused as she is.

"I... Why did you dance?"

"It's your birthday. I wanted to do something for you."

Sighing, I rub my hands over my face. I don't know how to have discussions about feelings. This is much more difficult that just shooting someone and being done with it.

"Did you actually want to dance, or did you do it because you thought I would want you to?"

"Both?" She shrugs her slumped shoulders. "I wanted to do something for you, and I thought you would like that."

"I fucking loved it, but I also hated it. You... I never want you to do something because you think I want you to, only do things you actually want to do." Please understand what I'm trying to say.

"I did want to, for you."

"I don't want you to do things for me, I want you to do things for you..."

Her lips part in surprise, then understanding washes over her face. Then, inexplicably, her mouth pulls into a thin annoyed line.

This upsets her?

"Why are you unhappy?"

"I'm not," her fingers fidget in her lap. "I just don't really know what kind of things I want to do. No one ever gave me permission to do something just because I wanted to."

"You don't have to decide right now. Just, when something comes up, something you would like to do, do it. Likewise, when you don't want to do something, don't. You are the Queen here; there is nothing you can't do."

"What if I want to dance for you?" Her lower lip pokes out.

My cock stirs. Fuck.

"I will build a stage in our bedroom."

Her head falls back, and she laughs, "So, you *were* jealous."

195

CHAPTER 37

 Kane

MY FINGERS DRUM against the table. I can name at least one hundred things I would rather do than this, including being set on fire.

Gideon called early this morning, he's on his way here for an impromptu meeting.

I don't like him under even the best of circumstances, but he interrupted while I was balls deep in Anaïs for the fifth time last night. I hate him more than normal right now.

It took everything in me to tear myself away from her this morning. Her soft breaths, her strawberry hair spread over the pillow, her lashes fanning her cheeks. She was so tired she barely stirred when I kissed her goodbye.

I bet she's still asleep, curled up in my bed, naked.

Zion is so hungover that I'm not sure he's even conscious.

His face is down against the conference table, and he hasn't moved in several minutes.

Looking at my watch, I decide to give him exactly one more minute. If he's not seated across from me by then, I'm leaving, and he can go fuck himself.

Thirty.

Twenty-nine.

Twenty-eight.

Fuck. The door clicks open, and he steps in, looking like the fucking Easter bunny in a pale blue suit.

Twenty-two seconds. I was so close.

"Good morning!" He has a big, stupid smile on his face, and I'm immediately uncomfortable. It's not only odd that he called this meeting, but it's more. There's more. I can see it in an instant by the smug look on his face.

"Why are you here? Our next quarterly isn't for two months." I'm not willing to play games with him. Whatever the reason for this bullshit meeting, he had better get to it. I'm in no mood to fake pleasantries.

He slides confidently into the seat across from mine. "I heard there is a new queen. I was hoping she would be here with you today."

I hum and drum my fingers again.

"I was wondering, what was her crime?" He stares at me with a hubris that makes my trigger finger itch. "What kind of crime does a lady have to commit to gain the attention of the King?"

I'm not sure if he's just being an arrogant bastard or if he actually knows something. His visit would suggest the latter. I assume he bribed someone for the files, or lack thereof. If he knows that she's not supposed to be here, I'm fucked.

"What do you want? You came all the way down here to talk about her?" Zion's voice is croaky and irritated. "Are

197

things really that boring up there that you have to come down here and waste our fucking time?"

"I was just coming to meet the woman that would rather live in hell with him than come live free up top, that's all."

Zion raises his head, and we make eye contact. Well, shit. He definitely has questions now.

"That's none of your business. What I do, what she does, and why, you don't need to concern yourself with that."

He lifts his hands in surrender, but that fucking smirk is still on his face.

"No need to get angry, Kane, I was only curious."

"What's that old saying about curiosity?" I look to my brother, whose lips are twitching upward into a menacing smile.

Gideon's brows furrow. "No need for threats, Kane."

"You don't think so?"

"No, I just wanted to meet the new queen." She's quite the looker from what I'm told."

The thought of them meeting makes my stomach turn.

"You may not think so but I'll warn you, I get positively violent at the thought of people's 'curiosities' when it comes to my woman." Something burns at the base of my spine. I can't put my finger on it but I want him gone. Now. I would love to rid the world of him completely.

He looks like he's regretting all of this. Good. He came here to rattle me, to scare me into making a mistake or revealing something I shouldn't.

"Do you have any actual business?" Zion is too hungover to deal with this.

"Next time I see you," I stand from my seat, "you need to be about business —your own fucking business. Keep your schoolgirl gossip to yourself. In the future, I might not be so willing to overlook this kind of blatant attempt at intimidation." Holding the door open, I gesture for him to walk through it.

With a scowl on his face, he walks toward me, stopping in the doorway in front of me.

"I wouldn't be so quick to threaten, Kane. You might be the King in The Underworld, but you aren't the only one here with an affinity for violence. You are not invincible. You would do well to remember that."

Something is coming, and he wants me to know that he's involved. His arrogance won't allow him to stay silent, to sit back and watch as the element of surprise leaves me at a disadvantage. He wants me to know.

"What the fuck was that all about?" Zion hardly waits for the door to close before turning to me.

"Anaïs, she, uh, " I don't even want to speak the words. "She didn't commit a crime. Her fucking father did, and he snuck her mother in. She was born here."

His mouth is hanging open in disbelief. For the first time in our lives, he's silent.

"How did you convince her to stay down here?"

Fuck.

"I didn't mention that she had any other option," I mumble under my breath.

"Yo! This is fucked!" He has the most screwed up moral compass of anyone I know. If he thinks I fucked up, I really did.

"I know alright."

"What's your plan here, man? Just to keep her locked in the house? You know that motherfucker will say something if he ever gets the chance-"

"I know! I fucked this up." I cut him off. I can't hear about how badly I ruined everything anymore.

"He has a big fucking mouth! He's probably told every

person he's come into contact with since finding out. This is a landmine, bro. You're screwed."

Everything boils over, and I see red. My fist pounds into the window until my rage is quelled slightly. I need to get out of here. I need to see her. The only thing that can truly calm me down is her. Whatever is coming, I need to protect her from it.

My mind races. Above all else, she has to be safe. I can't keep her safe if she fucking leaves me for lying to her.

The thought of her leaving me fills me with a feeling I don't understand. It's like I can't catch a breath. My heart is beating so fast, and the room is suddenly several degrees warmer.

Without a word, I run from the room. I have to get to her. To see her with my own eyes. She's still here. She hasn't left.

Every second of the ride home feels like an eternity. My chest is tight, I'm dizzy and nauseous.

As the elevator opens, my eyes find her immediately. She's standing in the kitchen, wearing my shirt. When our eyes meet, the smile slips from her face at the state of me. She sets her coffee down quickly and takes a tentative step toward me.

Everything hits me at once. Rage and fear, lust and guilt, protectiveness and love. I can't lose her.

CHAPTER 38

 naïs

HE LOOKS WILD. Like a wounded animal that's been cornered. His jacket is gone, and his shirt is disheveled over his heaving chest. His usually well-groomed hair looks tousled and tugged. The knuckles on his left hand are busted open, crusted blood drying over the wounds.

"Anaïs," his voice wavers, "I need you, baby."

I don't know what happened. I don't know why he's so frantic. Without hesitation, I'm running to him, pulling his large body into my arms. I'll offer him any comfort I can give.

His mouth finds mine in an instant. The kiss and tight grip of his hands are as panic-stricken as the rest of him. He's holding me like he's afraid I'll disappear.

Vaguely, I register that he's pulling down his pants, but

201

the kiss is too consuming, too hungry. Somehow he manages to pull his pants down enough to release his length between us. He lifts me up, bunching my shirt around my waist as I wrap my legs around him.

"Kane," I whimper against his mouth, "sit down."

His brows furrow, but he walks the distance to the sofa and sits with my body still over his. The concern on his face makes my heart constrict. Pulling myself up and off of his lap, I watch as his eyes follow my movements.

"Are you sore, baby? I'm sorry-" His eyes dart over my body like he's searching for injuries.

I shake my head 'no' and reach up, under his shirt that I'm wearing. As my panties drop down to my ankles, his body tenses. It only makes me want him more knowing how much he cares about how I'm feeling.

When I climb back over his lap, my naked core on top of his, he looks like he's short-circuiting.

Taking his hand, I press soft kisses to his fingertips and palm, then to his battered knuckles.

"No, baby," he tries to pull his hand away, but I hold tight. Looking into his eyes, I kiss the torn skin. My mind flickers back to all the times he's taken care of me, licked and kissed my tender, swollen skin, and the times he's gently washed me. I want to care for him the same way, to kiss his pain away, to show him the same love.

With each soft kiss, I can feel him twitching beneath me.

When I grind my hips down, a choked panting sound comes from the back of his throat.

With his hands still in mine, I wrap his arms around me. He quickly obliges me and holds my hips in his hands.

I drop my hands down between us, running them over his chest and stomach as I do. His muscles clench under my touch.

"I want to." My voice shakes, "I want to take care of you, to show you." I hope he understands what I mean. I wish I could tell him something dirty. I wish I wasn't too shy to tell him exactly what I want to do to him.

"Show me," he connects our mouths again.

His voice is different. He seems so vulnerable right now. I don't know what happened in his meeting, but he's not alright. His normally unshakable confidence seems to have been replaced with helplessness.

Pushing slightly on his chest, I make enough space between us to look into his eyes. I lift up, hovering my hips over him. When my fingers grip him, he drops his forehead to mine.

Forcing myself to be confident, to push my insecurities down and take care of him, I press myself down onto the tip. His grip is so tight that I can't move. I want to slip down further, but he's holding me still.

I bring my hands to his cheeks, watching him until he looks up from between us to make eye contact. He looks lost.

I feel his grip release, so I take the opportunity to sink down further. I can't help but gasp as my eyes flutter closed. My muscles strain and stretch. I didn't know it was possible to feel him deeper, but this is different.

Taking a deep breath, I drop down completely, letting my hips rest on top of his. His jaw falls slack, and he chokes on my name.

"I need you," his voice is strained. "Please don't leave me, baby."

I put my hands on his shoulders to steady myself, leaning forward to kiss his forehead. "I'm right here."

Our mouths meet, desperately moving together. He's buried inside of me; I'm in his arms on his lap, but we're not close enough.

"Anaïs," he begs, "God-fuck, please, baby. Please move; ride me. You feel so fucking good."

My core pulsates around him. His dirty words, the lust in his eyes, his hands on my body—everything comes together to create a perfect storm under my skin. It's hard to feel anything less than confident when he wants me so badly.

Using my grip on his shoulders, I rock my hips up, then slide back down, starting a slow rhythm that makes me shudder.

"It's so deep like this," I whimper, the pressure of my slow circles building.

I roll my hips faster, feeling his tip massaging me in a way that has my body shaking. A tight ball in the pit of my stomach knots together painfully.

"What the fuck?" He chokes as I bounce faster. The mind-numbing tightness in my stomach is too much to bear for another second. I move as fast as my hips will allow, rolling them up and slamming down onto him.

His head falls back, and the veins in his neck strain against his skin. With his eyes pinned shut and his jaw clenched tight. "Just like that," he pants.

My stomach is clenched so tight. A deep, throbbing ache is all I can think about. I have to go faster, I have to unravel this.

His hands drop from my hips and move behind him, supporting himself on the seat. When he thrusts his hips up to meet mine, I'm shattered.

Pleasure bursts through me like a dam breaking—not a trickle but a flood. My stomach clenches, and I feel myself clamp down on him so tightly that he freezes. A sound comes out of him that makes me shake.

I can feel him twitching inside of me, warmth filling me.

"Holy fucking shit," he grits through his teeth, slumping forward to press his face into my neck.

For a few minutes we don't move, we just sit, clinging to each other.

"Are you alright?" I whisper against his cheek.

"I just need you." He sounds so tired. The exhaustion is clear in his voice.

"I'm not going anywhere, baby," I let my fingers walk down his back, gently grazing his skin.

My body is slumped into his. His fingers glide over my back slowly, making it hard for me to keep my eyes open.

His phone starts to ring in his pocket, and we both groan.

"What?" he snaps. I don't know who is calling, but I can hear the faint mumbling of their reply.

"I need a minute," Kane growls and drops the phone onto the seat beside us. "I have to go. It's judgment day." He brings his arms around me.

"Can I come?"

He grabs my shoulders and presses me back to look at my face. He looks incredulous.

"You want to come with me to judgments?"

"Yes." I nod for emphasis. I want to be there for him. I can do it.

He studies my face for a moment before shrugging, "Of course, you can come."

"I can't promise that I won't get upset, but I want to be there with you."

We rush to change, fighting all the way down the elevator about the first aid kit I brought. I want to wrap up his hand while Declan drives.

"Fine," he pouts. "You can wrap up my hand."

"Thank you."

As I carefully wrap a bandage over his knuckles, a weird smile pulls at his lips.

"What?" I feel self conscious. Why is he looking at me like that?

"You called me baby earlier."

CHAPTER 39

 naïs

My strategy as we walk into the judgment room is not to look at the people there. I know what to expect this time. I'm going to keep my head down and sit beside Kane. I need to just rip off the band-aid. As difficult as it is for me to stomach, judgment is a part of his life, it's one of his responsibilities. Having him in my life makes this a part of my life too. The sooner I adjust, the better.

"Are you all right?" he whispers as Declan hands him a large stack of files. "If you need a break or you want me to stop, all you have to do is say so." He reaches over the armrest and takes my hand in his.

"First up," Kane's voice booms. "Clint West."

Kane chuckles, and my eyes jerk up from my lap. I didn't want to look, but I have to see why he's laughing.

The man that steps forward isn't like the rest of the

group. He doesn't look afraid. There is no emotion on his face at all.

"Clint," Kane's voice is low, "You're charged with assault."

The man nods his head but doesn't speak.

"You aren't going to try to plead your case? Cry self-defense… beg for your life?"

"It wouldn't make a difference," his voice is so calm.

"You work for Cohen Farly as a bartender, right?" I turn to Kane, watching him closely.

"Yes, I do."

"The bar opens this weekend. What have you been doing there in the meantime?" Kane's eyes narrow as he speaks.

"I've been there setting up the bar."

"Has Farly been present?"

"Everyday," his expression matches Kane's, incredulous and suspicious.

"In that time you never heard anything that might have been considered treasonous? Plotting, schemes…"

"I kept my head down and did my work. What Farly does or does not discuss with his associates is none of my business." He never wavers, never shows any fear if he feels it.

"Did you know about the attack?"

"No."

I might be gullible, but I believe him.

Kane nods his head and pulls his gun from his waistband. As he cocks the gun, I hum. It's quiet but he hears me.

He lowers his hand and turns to me, "You disapprove?" His brows are furrowed with concern. It almost makes me laugh. What did he think was going to happen? Of course, I disapprove.

"Mercy," I whisper just to him.

He groans loudly, the sound echoing in the marble room.

For a moment, he just stares at me. I should have kept

myself quiet, I shouldn't have interfered. Without a word, he turns away, placing the gun in his lap.

"My Queen demands mercy." He looks at the man who, for the first time, shows a bit of emotion. His brows raise in surprise for a second before he sets his face back to the stoic mask. "You may keep your miserable life, for now, but remember each time you draw breath, this woman beside me is the only reason your brains aren't splattered across the floor. Get out of my sight."

The man stands, nodding to me before he walks confidently out of the room.

When I turn to Kane, I find him scowling at me.

"What?" I shrink back in my seat.

"Why did you spare him? Why did he deserve mercy?"

"You wanted to kill him because he didn't know that Cohen was going to attack. Is it his job to know? He works in the bar. Does he work for you? Is he supposed to be collecting information? You can't just kill someone for not knowing something that they didn't know they were supposed to know." My nose crinkles at the end. "Does that make sense?"

He chuckles, deep and low, the sound vibrating in my panties, "I suppose it makes sense."

Clearing my throat I look away, the faces of the terrified crowd sobering me up quickly. There are at least forty people waiting for judgment. I let my body lean back against the chair. It is going to be a very long day.

"Next," Kane gestures for the next man to step forward.

My breath catches in my throat. I would recognize him anywhere. Leto. The man that grabbed me in The Playground, the man that hit me. He doesn't recognize me, I'm sure of it. He doesn't look fearful enough to remember that night.

"Tommy Leto," Kane looks over his notes, "theft."

"It wasn't theft, sir." His voice makes my skin crawl.

"It says here you stole from one of the women at The Playground." Kane looks over the notes.

"No, Sir. I refused to pay for a service. She didn't do what I wanted so I wouldn't pay, then she started screaming that I stole from her." His voice is as slimy as it was the last time I encountered him.

This man is evil. I could see it the night we met as easily as I see it now.

Kane looks at me expectantly, waiting for my judgment on this man. I'm sure he expects me to want him to be shown mercy also. When I nod my head 'no', his brows furrow.

He sits back in his seat for a moment, obviously deep in thought. Suddenly, he's standing and grabbing my arm. The heavy door slams closed behind us.

"Why?" he searches my face. "Why not mercy for that man?"

"He's bad." My answer is simple, it gives nothing away, but I can already see the rage building in him.

"How do you know he's bad?" His hand runs through my hair. He's being gentle, but I can feel his fingers tremble. He's trying to contain his anger long enough to let me explain.

"I've met him before. He tried to force me into one of the sex rooms at The Playground and when I tried to pull away, he hit me. Oksana helped me."

The muscles in his chest shake, and murderous rage glows in his eyes. He takes my face in his hands and presses his lips to my forehead, holding me there.

"Maybe you should stay here, baby," he whispers against my skin. His voice is hoarse and strained.

"I want to come with you." I know what's about to

happen. Well, I have some idea, at least. I want to be beside him.

He nods, gently leading me back into the judgment room. I take my seat, preparing myself for what I know is coming. I feel his fingers on my face, his thumb rubbing over my cheek.

He drops his hand and turns. It only takes him a few long strides to be standing in front of Leto.

Circling him quickly, he kicks the back of his knee, forcing him to the ground. In a burst of silent movement, he jams a long, thin blade into his neck, just below his ear. When he pulls it out, blood sprays across the floor.

Where did the knife come from?

Leto falls forward, clutching his neck.

Kane steps over his body and whispers something to Declan before walking toward me with his hand outstretched.

"That's enough for today," he kisses my palm.

CHAPTER 40

 naïs

THIS WEEK HAS BEEN ODD.

Ever since Kane came home from his meeting, he's been acting strangely. He is obviously still bothered by whatever happened, but he won't talk to me about it. He says that everything is fine and that I don't need to worry, but he clings to me at night.

He hardly sleeps, but when he does, he holds me so tightly that it's suffocating. Something has him worried. It's like he couldn't help himself that day. He let me comfort him, but now he's pulling away.

"What's wrong, Babydoll?" Oksana sweeps eyeshadow over her eyelid. "You're being so quiet."

I don't know what's wrong. That's the problem. He won't talk to me.

"Are you nervous about tonight?"

Yes. Very.

"A little bit," I distract myself by fastening the clasps on my shoes.

"Farly is a dick, but he's not about to sabotage his own party. He's been working for a long time to get this bar open. Tonight should be smooth sailing." She tries to comfort me, but the party really is the least of my worries.

"I'll be right back," I jump up and run out of her room before she can respond.

Kane and Zion stepped out earlier. I haven't heard them return, but he left Declan here. If Kane won't talk to me, I'll get my answers elsewhere.

"Declan," I find him sitting in the kitchen sipping coffee.

He chokes and stands up, "Yes?"

"Where is Kane?" I fold my arms over my chest. I hope it looks confident.

He looks nervous; "he had a bit of business before the opening tonight."

"Why didn't he bring you with him?" I narrow my eyes, watching the way his eyes frantically search around the room.

"I'm here to make sure that you are safe."

"Safe from what?" I step forward.

"Just safe, in general." He's lying.

I might not know much; I may not be savvy in the ways of The Underworld but I know a liar when I see one. My dad used to try to lie every time he lost all of his money at Hanzo's.

"Is Kane safe? Wherever he is, is he in danger?" I lean in, trying to force him to meet my gaze. He won't.

"He is safe-"

I cut him off, stepping forward again, "There is a threat though, right? Something is going on, I can feel it."

"You should talk to-"

"I'm talking to you!" I hold firm.

The truth is, I can't talk to Kane. Every time I try, he distracts me with sex. I fall for it every time. Poor Declan is definitely not the person I need to be asking about this, but he's the only option.

"Please, I can't. He will kill me," he's pleading with me.

"Call him," I point to his phone on the counter.

He hesitates but reaches for the phone, dialing and then placing it in my hand.

"Declan," Kane's voice is harsh and angry.

"It's me."

"Baby, what happened? What's wrong?" His tone is frantic.

"Where are you?" I'm getting answers this time, one way or another.

"I'll be back in about fifteen minutes." His tone is measured. He's being very careful.

"Kane, that's not what I asked."

I hear Zion laughing in the background. Kane mumbles something at him before sighing.

"I'll be home soon, and we'll talk, alright?"

"Fine." I hang up and hand Declan his phone.

I feel defeated. When he gets here, he's going to try to seduce his way out of this conversation, and my body is probably going to let him.

Walking into our room, I strategically sit in one of the armchairs, not on the bed. I'm going to need to be strong here. He's been so distant and stressed.

I run my hands nervously over my dress as I wait for him, smoothing out the wrinkles. When the elevator dings, my body hums. He's nearby. He's going to try to use his strong, powerful, perfect body as a distraction.

"Anaïs," he walks in and tosses his jacket on the bed.

I search his body, looking for injuries. I hate that I have to worry about that every time he leaves my side.

"Fuck, baby, you look incredible," he drops to his knees in front of me, his fingers grazing my ankle.

"No!" I press my other foot to his shoulder, pushing him away. "Don't try to distract me, Kane. Tell me what's going on!"

"Nothing, there isn't anything going on. You look beautiful, and we have to go to this stupid fucking opening event." He's lying. He's not making eye contact.

"You said I'm your equal, Kane. You told me that we're partners. Something is wrong, I can feel it, you're worried. You're hiding something from me."

His face falls, and he holds onto my foot.

"Fuck," he sighs and pulls his body up from the floor. "Gideon called that meeting as a thinly veiled threat. He wants me to know that he's after me. I don't know what he has planned, but something is coming. We're upping security everywhere, and I have some guys planted, just keeping an eye on the street."

"Wait, so Gideon is after you and Farly is after you?" My heart sinks.

"It looks like it. Until it's proven otherwise, I think they are working together."

"Why would Gideon be after you? He doesn't stand to gain anything from hurting you." I don't understand.

"He might see it as advantageous to have someone that he can control a bit better running things down here. He and I don't get along." There is something he's not saying, I can see it in his eyes. He doesn't want to talk about it. He kneels down again, running his hand from my ankle up to my knee.

215

My body betrays me, goosebumps spreading across my skin.

"Kane, we can't do this right now, we'll never leave the house," I hate my breathy voice.

"Would it be such a bad thing?"

"Maybe not," I can't control my whimpering as his hand slides higher up, over my knee to my thigh.

"Kane!" Zion yells from outside, "Put your monster cock away and let's go, motherfucker!"

"Oh my God," I bury my bright red face in his shoulder as he growls.

"I swear, I'm going to kill him one of these days."

CHAPTER 41

 ane

If anyone so much as blinks in my direction, I am liable to lose it and shoot them. Knowing that Farly is going to be slithering around is enough to enrage me on a normal day. Making my spectacularly foul mood even worse, Zion interrupted my attempt to talk Anaïs out of coming here altogether.

After our conversation, I feel even more agitated. I didn't want her to know about any possible threats. I want her eyes bright and her head free from thoughts of lurking shadows and danger.

I'll deal with the darkness. She stays, happy and unaware in the light.

Then, to top it all off, this fucking bar isn't a shithole.

Farly actually did a good job. As soon as we stepped inside, Anaïs was excitedly looking around at everything.

It feels like we're underwater. Not in a gaudy tasteless way. Everything is deep blue, and the lighting creates a ripple effect. The shadows move like waves over her skin, rays of light illuminating her, sparkling in her eyes.

Fuck, she's so pretty.

The dancers are wearing only pearly body paint.

"They look like mermaids," Anaïs whispers dreamily as she watches them.

I need a drink.

"Hey! You!" My attention quickly turns back to her.

She's smiling wide and waving at a woman. She looks vaguely familiar, but I can't place her.

"Hi, Anaïs!"

"Hi! You know, I never caught your name!" She blushes.

"I'm Victoria," she offers her hand.

Recognition finally hits me. She's Dec's girlfriend. That's probably something I should know.

"Jesus Christ, Vic, you didn't introduce yourself?" Declan scolds her.

"Shut up, I was really nervous." She looks at me quickly and then looks away.

"Wait, are you two together?" Anaïs points between them. I can see the wheels in her head turning as she puts the pieces together.

"Yeah, I just stopped by to see him for a minute actually," Victoria tells her, "it was really nice to see you again."

Dec takes her hand and takes a few steps away, talking quietly with her.

"I didn't know she was Declan's girlfriend!" She inches closer to me.

"That's not surprising, you didn't even know her name."

She rolls her eyes as Declan moves to stand behind our booth.

"Goodbye!" Victoria smiles, avoiding eye contact with me.

"You're not staying?"

"Oh, no. I just came to kiss Dec. It's our anniversary, and I wasn't-" Her voice dies, and she slaps her hand over her mouth.

"It's your anniversary today?" Anaïs turns to look at a panic-stricken Declan.

"Fuck, um," his eyes are shooting daggers at his girlfriend. "Yeah."

"Kane! He's working on his anniversary? Get a drink and sit down with us!" She waves sweetly at the waiter, "Spend a bit more time together."

Declan looks like he's about to pass out.

"No, we couldn't intrude. It's so kind of you to offer, but we really-"

"Please, sit. I hate the thought of you only getting two minutes together today. Please." She insists again.

"Sit." My voice comes out more harshly than I intended.

They both drop quickly into the booth with wide-eyed expressions.

"How long have you been together?" She asks, invested already.

"Two years," Declan answers nervously.

Their voices fade away as I watch Anaïs talk. She looks happy, laughing and smiling. Everything is out of focus except her. She is a light in the dark drawing all of my focus to her. I can't see anything else. Nothing else is worth looking at anyway.

The waiter brings over a deep sapphire drink, the

specialty cocktail. She takes a small sip, smiles, and takes another.

She slides closer to me, her hand resting on my thigh.

When my eyes catch hers, she's smiling up at me. She looks innocent, but I know better. She's taunting me.

Her fingers glide upward, only slightly, but it's enough to make my body tense.

"Are you alright, baby?" She leans in, whispering while sliding her hand up further.

I bite back a groan. She called me baby again.

"You seem tense," her fingers finally touch my desperate cock.

"I'm fine." I'm not fine.

"I was wondering if you might be ready to call it a night."

"You want to leave?" I feel like a kid on Christmas.

She nods her head and bites into her lip. Her fingers are tracing over the bulge in my pants.

As we stand from the table, Farly approaches with a broad smile.

"I'm so glad you found time to come!"

"Yeah," I pat his shoulder, "great place! Thanks for having us!" I usher Anaïs around him and to the door.

She giggles as we walk into the humid air outside.

"I think he was expecting a snarky conversation. He's still standing there stunned."

"He can stand there all night, I'm taking you home."

"Sir," someone calls from the alley. I stop and step in front of Anaïs. Declan steps around us, grabbing the man by the collar with one hand, his gun in the other.

Turning, I see it's the man from judgment, the bartender.

"Clint," Anaïs speaks from behind me.

"I'm sorry to bother you, but I need to tell you something. It's important."

I gesture to Declan to let him go.

"I overheard something I think you should know about." He looks at Anaïs, "I'm only telling you because she might get hurt, and I owe her."

I nod, waiting for him to continue. The thought of something hurting her fills me with a dread so deep it's likely to drown me.

"Farly's planning something. I don't know what it is, but he mentioned her. He was on the phone. I didn't recognize the caller's voice. The gist was that taking her out would be the easiest way to get to you."

My fists clench at my side.

"I'm sorry, I don't have any real details to give you. Just be on your guard. They're planning something, and she's the initial target."

I study his face for a moment, wondering if I can actually trust this man whose life she saved. Either he's a great liar or he's telling the truth.

"Clint," she calls out from behind me as he turns to walk away, "thank you."

CHAPTER 42

 naïs

"I'M SENDING you and Oksana with Declan up to the beach house until things blow over down here. I can't risk having you hurt." His words make me wince. He's never talked to me in that tone before. Authoritative and commanding, leaving no room for discussion.

He's pacing around the living room, pulling at his hair. I keep trying to grab him, to make him calm down and sit with me to talk about this, but he's too wound up.

The elevator dings and we freeze. Zion walks in with Oksana, their laughter immediately stops. After seeing Kane's face, Zion walks backward into the elevator, pressing the button repeatedly. Oksana stands frozen for a second before almost running past us, up the stairs.

"Pack your things." We aren't having a discussion, he's giving me orders.

222

"What about you?"

He sighs, "I can't come with you, baby."

"I don't want to go if you're not coming! Please, don't send me away!" A pit forms in my stomach.

"I'm not sending you away because I want you to go. I need to know that you're safe. I can't focus, I can't take care of this while I know that you're in danger!"

"Kane, don't whisk me away like a child." I feel like a child, like the little girl being scolded for making a noise. I don't have a voice here, my opinion doesn't matter.

"I'm not treating you like a child, I'm protecting you. This isn't up for debate! You are going, that's final!" The volume of his voice alone makes me jump.

Standing from the sofa, I walk quickly up the stairs, clutching the squirming puppy in my arms.

"Where are you going?"

"To my room. If you would like to have a discussion with me rather than yelling at me, you know where to find me." Turning on my heels, I walk down the hallway toward Oksana's room.

"Goddamn it," I hear him yell and the shattering sound of glass as I tap on her door.

"Yikes," she whispers with wide eyes.

Tears burn in my eyes. I told him not to treat me like a child, but now I'm crying. Squaring my shoulders, I try to keep my emotions in check. He isn't going to treat me like an adult if I don't act like one.

"You're allowed to cry," she rubs my shoulder before wrapping her arms around me. "What's going on?"

I tell her about Clint's warning through sniffles.

"I'm so angry," I whimper, leaning into her embrace. "It feels so helpless trying to talk to him. I know I'm not strong like he is and that I can't command the way he can, but I don't want to leave. If he is in danger, I won't be able to rest for a single moment. I'm not stupid enough to think that I would be able to keep him safe in any way, but I won't be here."

What if something happens to him?

"I don't know what to tell you. His word is law. I'm sorry." She lays her head on my shoulder. "If there is anyone I think he would listen to, it would be you, but-"

"How would he handle this?" I mumble out loud to myself.

Oksana snorts out a laugh. "He would probably shoot anyone that dared raise their voice to him, then he would simply refuse to leave."

I'm definitely not going to shoot him.

Jinx whines at the door, scratching to get out. I feel as trapped as he does.

None of this makes sense to me. I understand his fear, but he's not acting like himself. I haven't known him for very long, but he has been the picture of consistency in his behavior when it comes to me.

"Come on," she slides into her bed and holds her blanket open for me to get in beside her. "Get some sleep, you'll feel better in the morning."

I settle in beside her in the dark.

"Am I being unreasonable?" Why does he make me doubt myself like this?

"No, I understand where he's coming from, but you're not his daughter, your his, whatever you are. He doesn't get to command you the way he does with everyone else. I think he's just freaking out." She looks sympathetic.

I lie in bed, waiting for sleep that never comes. As much as I care for her, I don't want to be cuddled up to Oksana tonight. It takes every bit of restraint to keep me in this bed. I want to go to him, to hold him through the night.

The hours tick by slowly. With each minute, my misery grows.

Slipping carefully from the bed, I tiptoe across the floor and out into the hallway. The house is dark and quiet. All evidence of the loud, angry argument is gone, but the tension still hangs in the air. It's thick and heavy in my chest.

I see him before I can even step through the doorway. I see his dark silhouette against the lowlight shining in from the open wall of windows immediately. He's sitting on the edge of the bed, his head in his hands.

I stop, holding onto the doorframe, and watching him.

His hunched-over shoulders move slightly, up and down with each breath.

"Kane," my voice cracks.

He lets out a rough, heavy sigh before sitting up, "Anaïs."

We feel miles apart. The distance of only a few steps feels like a canyon between us.

"If something happens to you." he finally speaks. His voice is rough, the biting anger still very present.

"I understand that you want me to be safe, it's the same way I feel about you, but you can't just decide for me. I don't want to go without you. My opinions should matter."

"You're all that matters," he says, standing and steps toward me. "Why are you fighting me on this? I'm trying to protect you."

"I know you are, but," I rub my hands over my face. "For the first time in my life, someone, you, made me feel like I was more than what my dad raised me to be. You put me on a throne beside you and called me your equal. If I'm your queen, I don't intend to hide when things get rough. I want to stand beside you. As your partner, I want to shoulder the weight with you."

He groans and takes another step toward me. I finally see his face -fire blazes in his eyes.

"I shouldn't have yelled at you," he inches closer.

"No, you shouldn't have."

He chuckles, "You're not planning to let me off easy, are you?"

"That depends on how sorry you are and what you plan on doing to make it up to me."

He groans again, but this time it's not out of anger. Dropping to his knees in front of me, he presses his face against my stomach.

"I'm sorry, baby. I shouldn't have tried to demand you go." His voice wavers.

Running my fingers through his hair, I let my nails gently scratch at his scalp.

He hums and presses his face harder into me, bringing his hands up to rest on my hips.

"Can I show you how sorry I am?"

His deep rasping voice is like a vibration directly against my core. Slick heat pools in my stomach, and I tug at his hair.

"We still need to talk about this, Kane," I moan as his fingers dig into my skin.

"We will, baby, we'll talk about it all night until you're satisfied with my apology," he licks the fabric of my panties.

CHAPTER 43

 ane

I'VE HAD her on the floor, against the wall, bent over our bed, and in the shower. My body is insatiable for her.

We're in bed, her back to my chest as I gently pump into her. Our bodies are wrecked and exhausted, but I still want her. The frenzy is gone but the need is never satisfied.

Holding her close to my chest, her body wrapped around my cock, I'm painfully aware of the devastation that would ruin me if I lose her.

I can't lose her.

She whimpers, whispering my name into the quiet, her hand gripping the sheets as she tightens around me again. Fuck. It doesn't matter how many times we do this, it's never enough. She has a magic pussy and I'm fucking strung out. As I spill into the condom, my muscles sting from repeated tension.

227

If Farly thinks he can threaten her, he's got another thing coming. I will burn his life to ash around him. I won't stop until he's begging me for the sweet respite that death would bring. He fancies himself some kind of criminal mastermind, an outlaw. He has no fucking clue how dark this shit can get, and I can't wait to show him.

He's still alive because his father is well connected. I didn't care to expend the effort to squash him like the bug he is. Now, I fucking care.

As I pull out, I can tell she's already asleep. Fucked into peaceful oblivion.

After throwing the condom away, I sit on the end of the bed, watching her sleep. The sheets are tangled around her legs, and her hair is wild. The longer I watch her, the more my heart hurts. A sharp ache that grows with every breath.

There is a threat to her life, and she wants to stay here with me, to help me. Her pure heart is more than my black soul deserves.

I have to make today special for her. I have to remind her of the reason she gave me a chance. I have to make sure that she doesn't hate me.

Sliding into the bed beside her, I pull her soft body into mine, smelling her hair. She is everything that I am not. The darkness in me searches out her light. When I first saw her, I wanted her instantly. That feeling has only grown. I need her now. I'm sure I can't survive without her. Before her, I was existing, suspended in shadows, everything was empty.

It's only in hindsight that I can see how truly miserable my life was.

She rolls, turning her body, bringing her chest to mine. The peace on her face is baffling to me. Even in a shitstorm, she's calm. Weaving my hand through her tangled hair, I bring her head up onto my chest.

She hums, bringing her hand up to my chest. "Try to sleep, baby."

Baby.

Jesus Christ. My chest feels warm. No one has ever called me that. I might have been inclined to murder anyone that tried, but when she says it - tachycardia. I might be dying.

"Anaïs," I whisper in case she's already asleep again.

She lifts her head to look at me, waiting.

"Can I take you somewhere? I want to show you something."

"Of course," she kisses my chest, "right now?"

"Right now."

As she gets dressed, I call Dec to set my plans in motion. There isn't much time, this last-minute plan needs to be pulled together quickly or it will be too late.

Even as we rush, I watch her. The gracefulness of her movements, the sway of her hips, her hair hanging down to her waist. I commit every detail to memory.

"Are you going to tell me where we're going?" She smiles as we slide into the backseat.

"No."

She curls into me, resting her head on my shoulder as Declan maneuvers us through the streets. When he stops the car, she sits up, her brows raised.

"Your office?"

"Hurry, we're almost out of time." I quickly usher her out of the car.

The elevator takes us to the top floor. Her curious eyes roam around the lobby, trying to figure out where I'm taking her.

Down the long marble hallway, past my office, is a staircase.

"Roof access," she reads the sign on the door.

The hazy orange of sunrise has already started to glow across the sky as we reach the roof. A candlelit table is set up on the highest platform overlooking The Underworld.

"Wow," she's wide-eyed and breathless.

"It's not as pretty as the sunrise up top, but it's all yours."

"In its own way, it is beautiful." She wraps her arms around my waist.

We stand in silence, looking at the new day.

"K-Kane," she fidgets nervously, "I've been thinking about something."

I crane my neck down to look at her, waiting for her to continue.

"Well, I was wondering, I mean," she sighs, "this suddenly seems like a stupid thing to say out loud."

"Go ahead," I can't help but chuckle at her nervousness, but I'm intrigued.

"What if there was a place here for people that aren't so bad? I know they're all criminals, but what about Oksana? Or Declan and Victoria? Maybe there could be somewhere for them, for people that demonstrate a sort of moral compass." Her voice sounds unsure but the hope shining in her eyes makes me want to move mountains so that she can have this.

"Do you know why Declan is here?" I roll my lips into my mouth to hide my smile.

"Well, no, but..."

"A special place in hell," I can't hide my laughter anymore.

"You think it's stupid?" Her lips pull down into a frown.

"No, baby. I think your heart is too big for this place. If you wish to create a place for the well-behaved damned, it will be done."

"Really?" Her eyes light up.

"Of course."

All through our rooftop breakfast, she gives ideas and

details that she's considered for the project. Her passion and excitement make my heartache. She wants to reward the bottom-feeding miscreants of society with a place that is beautiful.

When we step into the elevator, she notices the torment I've been trying to hide.

"What's the matter, Kane?" Her fingers graze my cheek.

Fuck.

Pressing the emergency stop, I grab her, pulling her up into my arms. Slamming my mouth to hers, I kiss her, begging her with everything in me to forgive me. I can feel her trying to comfort me. Her hands cupping my face, her lips gentle and sweeping against my frantic, forceful mouth.

Everything is fucked, I've ruined it. She may never forgive me. The idea that this might be the last time she ever lets me kiss her burns at the base of my skull.

"Kane," she's pulling away, searching my eyes for answers.

"Please, don't hate me, baby." I hardly recognize my own voice as I press the button to continue to the lobby.

"Kane, you're scaring me. I won't hate you! What's happening?"

I squeeze her against me, appreciating the feeling of holding her so close.

When the door opens, Declan is waiting by the glass doors. She's still looking at me, trying to figure out what's going on.

"Sir," Declan opens the doors, and we step outside.

When she sees two cars, she stops and turns back around to look at me.

"I'm sorry, Anaïs. I can't allow you to be a casualty of my enemies. I'm doing what is best for you, even if it means you're mad. Be mad, but be safe. You're too precious to me. I heard you, I understand your position, but I can't let you stay."

Her chin trembles as she gives me a curt nod. I can see it in her eyes, she knows this is not a battle she can win. I'm surprised when she leans up on her toes and presses a kiss on my cheek before walking toward Declan.

I've never second-guessed myself. I've never made a decision and then lost sleep over whether or not it was the right one. Watching her walk away without so much as a backward glance is crippling.

My chest heaves as I watch the car pull onto the street and drive away.

CHAPTER 44

 naïs

OKSANA IS SITTING beside me in the backseat, her hand holding mine tightly. No one speaks. Declan's eyes meet mine several times in the rearview mirror, but he looks away quickly.

He dazzled me with sex. He spent the evening orgasming me into submission.

I'm angrier with myself than I am with him. How could I be such an idiot? I'm racking my brain trying to remember the specifics of our conversation. He apologized profusely, for yelling, for making me feel disrespected, for demanding instead of asking. Never once did he concede his position.

A humorless laugh bubbles up in my throat.

"I am such a foolish woman!" I swallow the painful lump in my throat.

"No, you're not. I don't want to play devil's advocate here, literally, but he's doing what he thinks is best to keep you safe." Oksana looks at Declan for help, but he averts his gaze.

"I thought I was getting through to him. I thought he was hearing me, and we were having a conversation between equals last night—all the while—he was planning this." I throw my hands up in the air. All the while, he was just satiating me into compliance, shutting me up long enough for preparations to be made.

I should have been expecting this. He isn't known to be a man that backs down. I just thought—I guess I don't know what I thought. Not so many days ago, he told me that he wanted me to do what I want to do. He made me feel that the power to make decisions about my life was in my hands. Now, clearly, I know that this is false.

The choice is mine as long as it aligns with what he wants me to do.

I shake the thoughts from my head and close my over-tired eyes. I need sleep.

"Shit," Declan mutters under his breath, and I feel the car change lanes abruptly. Jiji whines in the front seat like he can sense it, too. Something's wrong.

"Dec?"

Oksana is turned around, looking behind the car.

"Are we being followed?" She looks afraid as he swerves again, taking us off the main road.

A large black SUV swerves, barely making the exit.

"Fuck!" Dec starts pressing buttons on the console, trying to call for backup.

"Dec!" The car is coming up behind us too fast, it's about to run us off the road.

"I see it," he tries to move, but we're hit from behind. We lurch forward, skidding into a parked car.

"Fuck, fuck, fuck!" Declan jumps out and runs around the

front of the car to my door. The frame is bent enough that he can't pull it open.

He yanks the front passenger door open, pulling a gun from his waistband.

"Climb over the seat, both of you, take cover, and run. Don't fucking look back, just run. Get the fuck out of here!"

Ducking down, he uses the car for cover as he moves toward the back.

Oksana jumps into the front, grabbing Jiji. I follow her out, and we run toward an alley. We're in a desolate area with only broken-down cars and boarded-up buildings lining the crumbling street. If anyone was around, they ran as soon as trouble started.

The popping sound of shots being fired echoes behind us, breaking glass and bullets ricocheting off of cars. I drop down lower, the adrenaline pushing me to move through the fear.

I don't have time to stop and look, but by the sound of the bullets, we're very outnumbered.

Another black SUV drives up onto the sidewalk, blocking our path. The driver parks diagonally in front of the entrance to the alley, our best chance of escape.

Several men jump out, weapons drawn.

"Shit, Anaïs, run!" She pushes me back. The buildings all look abandoned. I don't see anywhere we can go but back toward Declan.

As I turn, I see him, and my heart sinks. He's wearing all black, so I can't tell where he's hit, but I know he's hurt. His posture isn't right; he's hunched down, one of his arms hanging limply by his side.

A loud gurgling scream echoes behind me.

A large man with a tattoo of a naked woman on his face has Oksana by the throat, holding a gun to her head. Her eyes bulge from the pressure he's putting on her neck. Jiji is standing at their feet, his tiny puppy barks, doing nothing to deter the men.

"Wait!" I turn to my side to look between the two groups of enemies. Bile rises in my throat.

Kane, where are you?

"I'll let her go right now if you come with us. No one has to get hurt." The man smiles, revealing gold teeth.

Oksana shakes her head, telling me not to listen, but the fear in her eyes sends a cold chill down my spine. It's like she knows she's about to die.

"We only want you, no one else has to get hurt." One of the men holding a gun to Declan calls out.

It suddenly occurs to me that Kane might be in trouble too. Maybe he's being attacked in a coordinated ambush. Looking out, past Declan, I search the road for any signs that he's coming.

"Ok, I'll come with you! Please, don't hurt them! I'll come!" I scream. I can't watch them be shot.

One of the men steps forward, reaching his arm out.

"No! Let them go first! I won't fight, I won't make this difficult. I'll be calm and quiet." I jerk back, stepping away from him.

"Drop your weapons," one of the men steps toward Declan.

He makes eye contact with me, his head dropping in defeat as he tosses his gun to the ground. The man kicks it away and steps forward, hitting Dec in the head with the handle of his gun. His body slumps forward, crumpled in the middle of the street.

Oksana is thrown to the ground as the man grabs my arm. My feet drag as he pulls me into the SUV, sliding into the seat beside me.

"I can see why he was so keen on keeping you, you sure are a pretty little thing," his fingers trace my cheek.

The adrenaline that had been pumping through me is fading. It's like my body is shutting down. I can feel the exhaustion wash over me, draining me.

We should have been together.

Is he even still alive? Will I ever see him again? Tears spill over onto my cheeks as I'm driven toward the border. Even now I hold out hope that he'll show up, that he will stop this from happening.

Kane, where are you?

BONUS CHAPTER

Zion

The bass vibrates through the speakers, shaking the ground beneath my feet.

Candy is on stage, her ass bouncing to the beat. As I stand, watching her thick curves ripple and shake, my mind wanders.

Fucking Kane has taken not one but two girls from me in just a few weeks.

Kitty. The name I gave to Oksana because her pussy is so good it had my ass ready to settle down. Not really, but she had me locked down for over a week, which is an impossible feat.

I wonder what she's up to tonight. My cock twitches just thinking about her dripping wet cunt.

Maybe I should call her?

I've never fucked anyone at Kane's house before. This could be a bucket list opportunity. I highly doubt Babydoll is going to be down to give my dick a ride any time soon.

Pulling out my phone I contemplate whether this will be worth the ass-kicking Kane will likely give me for laying pipe in his house.

Worth it.

"What do you want, Zion?" She already sounds over my shit, and I haven't even said anything yet.

"I've got a problem, babe. I need your expert advice."

She hums, "What's the problem?"

"See, recently I've felt the need to broaden my horizons. To open my heart to the possibilities of companionship."

"Is that so?" I can hear the smile in her voice. She knows I'm full of shit.

"Yes. I've decided that I want to start cuddling."

She snorts, "What are you calling me for? Go ahead and cuddle if you want to."

"I need help," I can hear her laughter. "I need a friend, someone I can trust, to teach me how to do it."

"Are you asking to come over?"

"Are you inviting me?" I'm pulling my jacket on and grabbing my keys before she responds.

"I can't have you out here embarrassing yourself. Come on over, I guess. I can teach you some techniques that will make you a top-notch cuddler in no time." Her voice is so soft and sexy.

"I'll be right there, be naked." I hang up before she can say anything else.

As I drive, my imagination runs rampant. If Kane isn't home, I would really love to fuck her on the balcony. Or maybe in the kitchen. He's got a sheepskin rug in his office. That might be too much.

As the elevator slowly brings me to the top floor, the anticipation grows. I haven't had sex in nearly twenty-four hours. A possible new record. Who better to break my fast with than Oksana?

As the doors slide open, I'm disappointed not to be met with her wide-open legs greeting me as soon as I step out.

"What the fuck are you doing here?" I spot Kane in the kitchen.

"I fucking live here, asshole. What are you doing here?" He's grumpy as usual.

"I'm here to see Oksana, you know, the second girl you stole from me."

He sets his glass down and glares at me, "Anaïs never belonged to you, so I didn't steal her."

"Tell me," I walk up a few steps out of striking distance, "how sound a sleeper is Anaïs, anyway? Things may get very loud fairly quickly."

He lunges forward, but my preplanning paid off. I'm able to jog up the stairs before he can land a punch.

I suppose since he is home, some of my ideas are going to have to be put on the back-burner for another time. Bummer.

Tapping her door I rock on my toes, excitement about all of tonight's possibilities running through me. I love fucking. I can't wait to be balls deep, drowning in Lake Oksana.

"Why aren't you naked?" She looks amazing, in a little sheer number that shows off her ample assets barely covering her.

"Wow, I'm glad you called. You really do need help. The first thing you should know about cuddling is that you don't have to be naked!" She quirks her brow at me in mock surprise.

"I think naked cuddling sounds better."

"Naked cuddling sounds a lot like fucking."

"We'll call it aggressive cuddling. My cock wants to cuddle the shit out of your pussy."

She throws her head back to laugh, and I take the opportunity to drop to my knees in front of her. Taking her by surprise as I press my face into her. Lake Oksana, so fucking wet. I press my tongue into her slit and lap up her delicious taste.

Jesus Christ. Nestled deep between her legs, my tongue runs over a smooth metal notch. Her ass is plugged.

Fuckin' Oksana, she never disappoints.

Taking one of her legs, I place it over my shoulder, giving myself better access to her. I consider myself a master when it comes to all things related to pussy. Long, squelching licks, tongue flicks, nips, sucking, kissing, I don't leave any flesh untouched. By the time I'm finished, she's hoarse and raspy, screaming my name.

When I pull my face from between her legs, I'm soaked. My favorite kind of bath. If you don't leave the bed completely filthy, does it even count? I think not.

"I want you to ride me, bounce on my cock so I can watch your tits bounce," I grab her and pull her toward the bed. She offers no resistance, swinging her leg over me to settle on top of my body.

With one hand around my shaft, I hold myself in position beneath her.

My stomach clenches as she drops down, taking all of me in one swift motion. Watching my cock disappear into a tight, wet cunt is the single most glorious sight there is. The tight suction of her walls stretching around me makes me groan.

I'm always loud during sex, I don't ever hold myself back from fully letting go and feeling everything. I'll admit that I'm being slightly louder than normal, hoping to annoy Kane.

"Fuck, thats it," I rip the little camisole off of her body so I can see her with nothing, even sheer fabric, in the way. "You're so goddamn perfect. The way your tight little cunt is squeezing me."

"You feel so good," she moans, her head falling back, exposing the curve of her neck to me.

Reaching up, I grab it, squeezing slightly. The action makes her clench around me. The tight pressure, the rippling tension—it makes me delirious.

She rocks faster, her hips moving up and down and in tight circles. Why did I ever stop fucking her?

"Jesus Christ!" I feel the pressure building, my dick swelling, the fire burning in my spine.

"Oh, God! Zion," she tenses again, her body seizing.

"Come all over my cock," I thrust upward, fucking her through her orgasm. It's too good, too wet, too fucking tight. I jerk inside of her, squeezing her ass in my hands.

I think I blacked out for a second because when I come back to reality, she is still seated on my cock with her head on my shoulder.

"I fucking love cuddling," I nip at her neck. "Want to try to cuddle in a different position?"

"What position?"

"It's called the wheelbarrow."

After the wheelbarrow, the seashell, the butter churner, the pinball wizard, and the valedictorian, my cock is empty, rug burned, and exhausted.

With Oksana tucked into bed, fast asleep, I sneak out for a drink. If I don't get some fluids, I'm going to pass out.

"Why the fuck are you naked in my fucking kitchen?" Kane growls quietly. He looks like he's about to make good on his usual threats of shooting me.

"Jesus!" I nearly spill my drink, "Why are you lurking around in the dark like a freak?"

"I'm not lurking around, this is my house. I came to get... Why am I explaining myself to you? Put some fucking clothes on. Better yet, go home!"

I notice that his hair is kind of sweaty, sticking to his face and neck, and he's only wearing briefs.

When a leering smirk stretches across my face, he huffs and rolls his eyes.

"Looks like both of the Azrael boys put in work tonight," I bump his shoulder.

"Get the fuck out of my house," he rolls his lips into his mouth, trying to hide his smile.

I wonder if it would be too much to try to convince him to tag team—probably.

NOTE FROM THE AUTHOR

Dear Reader,

I wanted to take this opportunity to thank you. Writing books is my dream, and knowing that you've taken the time to read them means everything to me. I can't express enough how grateful I am for your support. If you enjoyed the story, it would mean the world if you left a review on Amazon or Goodreads. Your thoughts help other readers discover the book. Even a few words make a huge difference! If you're not able to, that's okay—I'm just happy you're here. Thank you for being a part of this journey with me. I appreciate you more than you know.

With gratitude,
Myranda

ALSO BY MYRANDA RAE

Contemporary

When I Whisper His Name - A Big Brother's Best Friend Romance

Unplanned - A one-night stand turns into an office romance

Lewd & Lascivious - Lawyers, office politics, and a book boyfriend to die for.

The Void He Fills - An artist and her physical therapist do more than heal her body.

Pink - A workplace romance with a twist.

What's Done in the Dark - The Ruler of The Underworld finds true love in the Hades & Persephone retelling.

Paranormal/Shifter

Alphas, Kings & Playthings - She has trained for years to be the Alpha Kings breeder. But then she meets his brother...

Hardest to Love - A vampire prince falls for a human woman, and it's happily ever after—for a while.